Rayne Comes to Town

Dannie Marsden

Affinity
eBook Press
NZ

Acknowledgments

Acknowledgements: I want to thank Nat and Julie for the time they have spent in helping me with this venture. Affinity eBooks for the faith and trust they have in me and a special thanks to Mel for the endless support and help she has offered throughout, as well as the calming voice when I'd hit panic mode.

Dedication

This book is dedicated to the love of my life Heidi, who tirelessly encourages me to aim higher. Heidi thank you for all you do and know that I love you with all my heart.

Prologue

Rayne Mathews stood in her father's study, her back rigid with anger.

"You will marry Martin Sinclair in a week, girl, it's all been arranged."

"But, Father, I don't know him well nor do I love him. His breath smells awful and I can't stand it when he touches me."

"You will grow to love him. He is a well-respected man in this community and he needs a wife. You are old enough to marry and he has promised to make you a decent husband."

"Father, please..."

"There will be no more said on the subject."

"Father, please don't make me do this," she begged.

A hand struck her on the left side so hard that she saw stars.

"Do not argue with me. You will do as I say without question."

Rayne realized then that another beating was on the way if she said one more word. But she couldn't help herself.

"No, I won't," she said,

By the look in her father's eyes she wasn't at all sure she would walk away from this one, let alone live to marry any man. When her father forced her backwards, reaching for her, she bumped into the heavy desk. She reached behind, feeling around for something with which to defend herself. Her fingers wrapped around the first solid object she could find—a heavy paperweight. Without conscious thought, her arm rose up and came down hard against the side of her father's head.

She hadn't meant to strike him as hard as she did but she had been terrified and tired of the beatings. Her father went down and blood poured out of the gaping wound on the side of his head. As reality invaded her mind, so did panic. She moved around the desk, opened a drawer, and took the stack of bills and loose coins that she saw there.

It was fortunate for her that no one else was in the house. She dashed up the stairs to her brother's room and grabbed a pair of his trousers, a shirt, long johns, and a pair of socks. She raced into her bedroom, quickly took off her dress and petticoats, threw them on the bed, and pulled on her brother's clothes.

Back downstairs, she raided the kitchen by throwing food in a rucksack and took her father's guns, holster, and Stetson off a coat rack by the door. It wasn't long before Rayne, decked out for travel, was out in the stable.

"Hey, boy, do you want to go with me," Rayne whispered.

Apache, a horse she'd raised since he was a colt, nudged her.

"You'll get a carrot later, boy. Right now we need

to put some distance between us and Boston." Rayne quickly hefted a saddle over the big horse and once the cinch was in place she put the bridle in his mouth and over his head.

After grabbing a duster off a peg, she led her horse out of the stable. Just as she was about to mount Apache, she spied the family's laundry floating in the breeze. She liberated a few more items of her brother's clothing before she put a foot in a stirrup and got up on Apache.

Rayne studied the only place she ever knew as home and stopped for a moment as she remembered her father's still body lying on the floor of his study.

"I have no choice now," she whispered.

She quietly made her way down the path that led to the road and away from her family home.

†

Rayne, wearing the duster, leaned against a tall oak as rain pummeled against her. The only good thing about the rain was that her trail would be harder to follow. Now she sat in the dark, shivering with one of the revolvers in her hand, waiting for someone to challenge her or a wild animal to attack her. She had never been out on her own and she needed to draw on what she had read to survive. And even more troubling, her father's death at her own hand kept replaying in her mind. But there was no way she'd marry Martin Sinclair. Her plan originally was to leave her home heading for Wisconsin and the home of her Uncle Luke and Aunt Martha. She knew that they would keep her safe and not send her back to Boston—killing her father was never part of that plan

She had been traveling the rutted road that the wagon train she knew had left two days earlier was following. She hoped to catch up to it and travel with them. That would keep her out of harm's way until she could get her bearings and make a firm plan about what to do next. At that moment, she knew where she was going but had no idea how to get there. The wagon train was her only hope.

After four days of hard riding and very little sleep, Rayne let out a sigh of relief when she saw the billowing white tops of the wagon train. She made sure none of her long hair was showing beneath the rim of her hat and urged Apache forward.

†

"Hello there," Rayne said.

The wagon master turned. "What do you want, boy?"

"I was hopin' I could ride along."

"If you're lookin' for handouts we ain't got none."

"No, sir, I'm just lookin' to ride along. Maybe help out if Indian's attack."

"Have you ever fired a gun, boy?" The man gave Rayne a once over.

"Yes, sir, I'm a right good shot." Rayne mentally thanked her Uncle Luke for teaching her how to shoot a gun. Her father was against it but Luke paid him no mind and had taught her anyway.

"You can ride with us if you like but I'll not stand for you takin' from the others."

"No, sir, I won't. Thank you."

The wagon master let out a grunt before slapping his horse's hindquarter and galloping away.

That night, Rayne made a campfire and ate the last of her food before lying down on the ground with her head resting on her saddle and the horse blanket pulled over her shoulders. For the first time since she ran away, Rayne slept and the dreams that had haunted her ever since she killed her father did not wake her that night.

For the next three weeks, Rayne rode at the back of the wagon train. She watched for plumes of dust coming behind her signaling a group of horses galloping to catch up. In another month, they would arrive in St. Louis and she would leave the wagon train and head north toward Wisconsin following the Mississippi River.

Without food, Rayne asked some of her fellow travelers for something to eat by offering them money. Some gave her scraps but most said they didn't have enough for their own families. A man, who had broken his arm when a wagon wheel ran over it, offered Rayne food in exchange for helping his wife and daughters set things up when they stopped for the night. That gave Rayne a place by a warm fire each night along with a fully belly.

"Rayne," Margaret Richardson said.

"Yes." Rayne looked at the slight girl who was two years younger than she was.

"Do you think California is the Promised Land?"

"Well, I think the Promised Land is heaven and from what I've heard others say, it is heaven and more."

"Then why aren't you going there? I heard my papa tell Mama that he hopes you go with us and marry me when we get there."

Rayne pulled her hat further down on her head. The thought of Wilber Richardson wanting to marry his daughter off reminded her of the father she had killed.

"Well," Margaret said. "Don't you want to marry me?"

Unable to speak, Rayne just looked at the girl and gulped in air.

"What's going on here?" Wilber asked.

"We were just talking about California and if it was the Promised Land." Rayne was grateful for the man's intrusion.

Wilber ruffled his daughter's hair. "Of course it is, child. That is why we are going there. Go and help your mother with the meal."

"I need to take care of the horses." Rayne nodded at the man and quickly walked away. The hair piled inside her hat itched and she needed to find a place to bathe and wash her hair.

If he only knew who I am, he'd never want his

daughter to have anything to do with me.

She unhitched the horses from their harnesses and hobbled them near the wagon. She moved to Apache and removed the saddle from his back.

"It's time we move on, boy. I heard them sayin' there's a town north of here. Tomorrow we will head that way and maybe they will have a bath place there. I sure can use one."

Rayne left her horse and went to the fire burning brightly next to the wagon. Yes, she knew it was time to go.

†

The town was just like all the others that she'd seen in her travels—dusty and busy. The main street was full of cowboys on horses and wagons pulling heavy loads. She saw some of the men from the wagon train going into the mercantile and avoided them. Her eyes landed on a sign. *Baths 5¢.* She guided Apache to the hitching post in front of the bathhouse.

"I need a bath," Rayne said when she entered the building.

A man sitting behind a tall desk looked up and grunted. "That'll be a nickel. If you want a private bath it'll be two bits."

Rayne gulped at the price. "That's mighty steep."

"Take it or leave it." The man shrugged.

"I'll take it." She reached in her vest pocket and pulled out the coin. "That is a hot bath with soap right?"

"Yep. Come back in an hour and it will be ready for you."

Rayne held back the coin.

"You don't pay me now you won't get the bath."

The coin bounced on the desktop. "I'll be back and it better be ready."

†

The bath was luxurious. Ever since she'd left her home, Rayne had only washed when she wandered away from the wagon train and found a stream to rid her body of the grime of the trail. It was bad enough when each morning and night she'd have to find a bush to hide behind to relieve her bladder. Now, she slipped deeper into the tub full of hot water relishing the feeling of being clean again.

In clean clothes, Rayne stepped out onto the wooden walk and surveyed the street. She spied a hotel with a cafe and headed toward it. A good hot meal and a soft bed to sleep in beckoned her. She would stay there one night then head north toward Wisconsin and her aunt and uncle's place in Willow Springs.

Rayne entered the eating establishment and looked around. Except for two tables with people around them, the place was empty. She headed for the first empty table she saw and sat down. Without thinking, she took off her hat and her hair floated across her shoulders.

"What'll you have, ma'am?"

"Steak, potatoes, and pie." Rayne looked at the woman and smiled. "I'm really hungry… been on the road for days."

"I'll make sure you get an extra thick steak."

"I'd appreciate that." Rayne watched the young woman walk away with her eyes fixed on her backside. The girl had long blonde hair and a pleasant looking face and when she had heard her voice and looked up, the familiar stirrings she always associated with women filled her body.

When the woman returned with her food, Rayne felt a blush heat up her cheeks. "Thank you. It looks delicious."

"We have apple and cherry pie. Which one would you like?"

"Apple, please."

When Rayne looked at the woman she saw something she'd only ever seen in Martin Sinclair's eyes— desire. "My name is Rayne."

"Hello, my name is Alice." She rested a hand on Rayne's shoulder. "You stayin' in town long?"

"Got a room here for the night…after that I'm heading north."

"I'll get your pie."

When Alice returned she set the plate with the pie in front of Rayne and leaned across her to get the empty plate. "You sure were hungry." Alice's breast skimmed across Rayne's back.

Rayne swallowed hard as she inhaled the sweet water perfume that she associated with another girl she once knew. "Yeah, I sure was."

"I finish up here around seven if you'd like to visit some more." Alice smiled. "We could meet in your room."

Rayne couldn't move. She could feel her heart pounding so hard that she wondered if it would burst. "Okay."

"Good I'll see you then." Alice looked around the room. "Looks like we're alone."

She leaned in and kissed Rayne's cheek. "I *will* see you later."

✝

Rayne sat on her bed waiting for the knock she hoped would come and was terrified that it would not. The feelings that the kiss on her cheek induced had her body humming in anticipation. She had no idea what would happen but she wanted the experience. No one had ever made her feel that way and she wanted more. When the knock finally sounded, she felt the tightness of her private parts reach new heights.

"Hi."

Alice walked past her and ran a finger down Rayne's cheek. Once the door closed, she moved so she was standing in Rayne's space.

Rayne, tried to squelch her rapid breathing but just one look from Alice made the rate escalate.

"It's okay, sugar, I won't hurt you." She ran her fingers along the buttons on Rayne's shirt. "Why do you dress like a man?"

The need to tell someone, even a stranger, her story was overwhelming. "I…ran away from home and I don't want them to find me. Dressing like a man gets me in places being a woman wouldn't," Rayne blurted out.

"You make a very handsome man but to tell the truth, I'm glad you're a woman." Alice leaned in and kissed Rayne.

Rayne jerked back.

"You've never done this before have you, sugar."

Rayne shook her head.

"Then let me show you."

Rayne willingly let Alice undress her before she took her hand and lead Rayne to the bed.

✝

Rayne woke the next morning and smiled as she recalled the night before. Before the night with Alice, she had no idea what it was that she had craved all her life. Alice had left her sated but wanting more.

"Sugar, I need to get home to my husband and children." Alice had smiled at her eagerness.

"Don't go," Rayne had begged.

"As you will find with your life, sugar, you have to hide who you are by marrying a man." Alice kissed Rayne.

"I won't ever marry a man." Rayne got out of the bed and pulled Alice to her. "Come with me and I will be your husband."

Alice shook her head and pushed away. "That's not how it works, Rayne."

She smoothed her dress. "It is how life is. You can either accept it or watch as people cover their mouths and whisper about you being unnatural."

"I don't care."

"You will." Alice gave Rayne one last kiss and opened the door. "Be careful out there, sugar, and have a safe trip to your uncle's place."

Naked, Rayne sat on the bed and considered Alice's words. "I will never marry."

She crawled under the covers, breathed in Alice's scent, and wrapped her arms around a pillow. Just as sleep overtook her she smiled. "I had no idea."

✝

For the next two months, Rayne made her way to Willow Springs. In each town she visited, she would check the wanted posters and never found any with her name. She'd visit the local saloon, take her hat off, and let her hair flow to her shoulders. When she revealed herself to be a woman, she found that many of the working girls in the saloon would fight over who would be the one to take Rayne upstairs.

Chapter One

The tall, lone figure sat astride a large bay looking out over a vast area with a sprawling, riverbend town centered in it. The sun shining high in the sky was already too hot for most and thoughts of a nice river bath, or some shade were teasing the woman in the saddle.

"What I wouldn't give for a cold stream right about now," she said aloud.

The bay snorted and shook his head.

"Yeah, I know," she responded. "Come on let's get goin'. If all goes as it should, we'll hit town by sundown. That means a nice stall with fresh hay for you and a hot bath, home cooked meal, and soft bed for me. Maybe even a beer if there's a decent saloon."

The bay nodded and struck the ground with his front foot.

Rayne laughed and shook her head in amusement before giving the horse a gentle nudge with the heel of her boot. Off they went down a slope, moving as one. With a few stops now and then to rest the bay and give her a break from the saddle, they eventually made it to the town just before sundown as Rayne had predicted.

The town was like every other she had been in during her travels. The only difference—on the outskirts of this town, stood a small house and grounds that that belonged to her aunt and uncle. As she rode into the town, she looked for the hotel, and the livery, knowing finding those would make her happy. A little way into town she spotted what looked to be a saloon, judging by the way all the dusty, rowdy men were going in and coming out. Weary from her journey, Rayne decided to try this establishment first. She rode up to the hitching post that stood in front and tied her horse to it. She swung her leg over the tall animal and finally, her foot touched solid ground. She pulled her hat low over her eyes, adjusted the gun belt she wore around her hips, and walked with confidence into the establishment. Like any other saloon, the minute the swinging doors opened and she walked in, the sounds of laughter, music, and empty mugs slamming down on the bar assaulted her ears. With a self-assured swagger, she made her way to the bar.

"What can I get for ya, mister?" The short man behind the bar asked without looking.

"I'll have shot of whiskey," she replied in a husky voice.

The bar keep looked up. "Comin' right up."

"Where might I find a decent priced room and bath, and get a good meal?" Rayne asked.

"Miss Bessie serves a fine meal three doors down and her rooms are two bits."

"One last thing, where can I find the livery?"

"Down the street take a left and it's at the end. Ralph should still be there."

"Thank you kindly." Rayne swallowed the amber liquid, tossed out enough coins to cover the drink, turned, and walked out the swinging doors.

Once she grabbed the reigns off the hitching post, Rayne walked to the side of the bay, mounted then led the horse down the road toward the livery. As she rode, she spied the big building at the end of the road bearing a livery sign. When she reached the entrance, Rayne dismounted, and with reins in hand, walked inside.

"Howdy, what can I do for ya?" the man asked.

"Lookin' for a stall and a bucket of oats for Apache here."

"Got one open off to the left there," he said as he motioned with his chin before walking over to Rayne, and reaching out his hand "Name is Ralph."

"Nice to meet ya, Ralph." She extended her hand and shook his. "Name is Rayne and this here is Apache."

Ralph reached out and petted the large bay, which nodded his head and nudged the farrier. Ralph took a good long look at Rayne as she started to un-strap the saddle and bridle. "You look familiar. Been in these parts before?"

"Years ago when I was a small sprout. I was visitin' my aunt and uncle."

"Mathews. You're Luke Mathews' kin, ain't ya?" Ralph took off his hat and scratched his head. "I can see the family resemblance."

"Yeah, I am." Rayne continued to take care of her horse.

"I'm real sorry about their passin'. Luke and Martha were real good people."

He eyed Rayne. "You come to stake your claim? I know the local attorney, a fella named Benton, goes out there every once in a while to check that the place is in good condition. Course all the cattle was sold to cover the burial expense and legal fees. I understand that what little was left was put into an account for Luke's kin".

Rayne, stunned by the words Ralph uttered, could only stare at the man in disbelief.

"I thought you knew and that's why you'd come here."

"They're dead?" Rayne shook her head.

"I'm right sorry for saying it the way I did."

"What happened to them?"

"It was the influenza that took 'em. Came into pneumonia, it did."

"When did this happen?"

Ralph scratched his head again. "Near as I can recollect it was about two months ago…maybe longer."

"Thanks. Do you know if…can ya tell me if it was quick?"

"Doc Adams could tell ya more… you can find him over at Bessie's right about now. You ask me, them two might as well get hitched. Shoot, neither of them can see straight when the other is around."

"Getting' hitched isn't for everyone, ya know," Rayne said quietly.

Still stunned by the news, Rayne finished brushing Apache down. She tried to make sense out of the news. *They were all I had…where am I going to go now?*

"How much for the night?"

"That'll be a bit for the night, includes bucket of oats in the mornin'."

Rayne reached into her pocket, pulled out a coin, and handed it the young man. "Much obliged. I'll be back in the mornin' to pick him up. Thanks for tellin' me about my kin." She gave the man a weak smile. "You have yourself a fine evening, Ralph."

"Thank you." Ralph pocketed the money, "Welcome to Willow Springs. Guess you will be livin' here now."

Rayne just nodded. *Uncle Luke probably left his place to my father not knowing I killed him.* "Who'd you say was looking after the place?"

"Mark Benton. He has a place near the sheriff's office."

"Thanks, Ralph, I'll see you in the mornin'" Rayne put her hat back on and walked out heading down the street toward the dining room.

Rayne walked into the dining room and looked around. Her heart was heavy and when she saw several people looking at her with their hands covering their mouths while they talked, she snickered. *Isn't that what Alice told me would happen.* With a shake of her head, she moved further in the room looking for a table. While she stood there, she overheard two women speaking.

That's her, the resemblance to Luke is amazing, Mavis. They said she was a woman. I've never seen a woman dressed like that. She won't last out there very long since every man around wants her land.

Rayne didn't understand the comments. How did they know who she was and why she was there? She never thought that she bore any resemblance to her uncle yet two people now said it was so. She looked at the two women and cocked her head in question—they immediately looked away.

Rayne continued to scan the room for somewhere to sit when a woman walked up to her with a big smile. "Well hello there and welcome. You must be Luke and Martha's kin. Bet your hungry and tired, come on let's get some food into you and then I'll have Jessie show you to your room and get you a bath. I'm Bessie, by the way. Heard about your arrival, and took the liberty of getting you a room already. Now what would you like? Judgin' by how scrawny you are, you'll need a nice thick steak, some fried potatoes and a nice cup of coffee. How does that sound?"

Rayne immediately liked the woman, and broke out in a smile before she remembered the passing of her aunt and uncle. "Did you know my Uncle Luke and Aunt Martha?"

"Sure did, honey. They were just real good people." Bessie looked at her. "You didn't know did you?"

Rayne shook her head. "Not until Ralph at the livery told me."

"Oh, I'm so sorry. We've been expectin' you for months now so I assumed you got the news and came here."

"I was fixin' on visitin' them, not findin' em

dead."

Bessie patted Rayne's arm and showed her to a table. "Now you sit right here and I'll see to it that you get a real good meal."

She started to leave then turned back. "Pay no mind to those busy bodies."

Rayne was dusty, tired, and hungry. And she could feel the eyes of everyone in the dining room staring at her, most of them probably not realizing she'd just heard about the death of her aunt and uncle. In her travels, she'd been in enough small towns to know that news traveled like wildfire. Here she was in Willow Springs, a place she'd visited as a child and had loved, feeling sad and alone.

From the comments she'd heard other make, it sounded as though the people were expecting her and not her father. *How can that be? Surely, the ranch should have passed on to my uncle's brother...my father who is dead.* Just as her coffee arrived, she heard someone behind her clear their throat and she turned and looked up to see a tall man standing next to her with a handsome, rakish smile.

"May I help you?" she asked.

"I don't mean to interrupt your dinner, just wanted to introduce myself and welcome you. I'm Jeremiah Sprigs; you must be Luke Mathew's kin."

"Name is Rayne. It's nice to meet you, Mister Sprigs." She studied the man as he held his hand out waiting for her hand. She did not take it

"Yes, well...." He cleared his throat again. "Welcome to Willow Springs. If you need anything...help with the ranch, someone to show you around town…a dinner companion…feel free to contact me. I'd be honored to help you out." Jeremiah said.

"Noted." Rayne picked up her coffee consistently staring at the man who nodded, abruptly turned on his heel, and proceeded to leave the dining room. In his haste, he nearly knocked Bessie down.

"Oh dear, not even here a day and already the vulture is circling. So sorry you had to experience him on your first evening in town. Trust me when I say that we are not all like him," Bessie said.

"He was just offering his services as a dinner companion if I should feel the need."

Rayne frowned, creasing her forehead. "Um, do all the snakes around here try to be charming?"

Bessie placed a thick steak and pan-fried potatoes in front of Rayne.

"Well, no. Jeremiah Sprigs is one of a kind I'm pleased to say. Lord help us, he does seem to think he is God's gift. He is more like a wart on a toad than the Lord's gift to anyone."

Rayne choked on the sip of coffee she had just taken. "Bessie, I do believe I like your sense of humor. Might I be able to talk you into resting your feet for a minute or two and give me the low down on who to avoid in this town?" Rayne flashed her most charming smile.

"Well it doesn't seem to be too busy right now. Don't mind if I do. My, my, talk about a charmer. Why I believe you could talk the skin right off of a snake if you set your mind to it." Bessie laughed as she sat down.

"Well, Bessie, I would surely try to give that snake a run for its money."

Rayne smiled before her face grew somber. "I understand that a fella named Benton is lookin' after Uncle Luke's place."

"Mark is a fine man…he's the only lawyer we got in Willow Springs. He's been takin' good care of the place so it would be ready when you arrived."

"I don't get it."

"What?"

"How everyone around her seems to know me and why I am here. I came to visit my aunt and uncle without telling anyone. How do you know it is me?"

"It's a small town and we all knew that Luke left his place to you."

"He what?"

"After Luke and Martha died, Sprigs was talking about the bank sellin' the place. Mark, told him that the place belonged to you and he sold the cattle so he could make sure the bank wouldn't take possession. Luke left a will givin' you his place."

Rayne's eyes widened so much she knew she looked like an owl. "I can't imagine that."

"Neither could Sprigs. He said no woman should be runnin' a ranch…that it was a man's job."

"Sounds like I need to meet that lawyer tomorrow."

Bessie patted Rayne's hand. "Let me get you some more coffee and a piece of apple pie."

Rayne watched the woman go and a smile curved

her lips. *I like her. She seems genuine.*

After pie and more conversation, Rayne stretched.

"Thank you for the mighty fine meal, Bessie. I reckon I've kept you from your work long enough, I think I'll head on up to my room and that hot bath you mentioned

"Of course, sweetie. Come with me. I'll fetch Jessie and she will show you to your room and help with your bath. You know, with you in town, Willow Springs just got a whole lot more interesting."

Chapter Two

The morning sun shone brightly into her window, signaling the new day. With a stretch and a deep yawn, Rayne slowly swung her feet over the bed and onto the floor. Feeling better than she had in weeks, she got dressed and headed down for breakfast. She walked into the dining room and grinned broadly when she saw Bessie heading her way.

"Good mornin'. How did you sleep?"

"Like a log, I have to say. Don't think I've ever had a bed that felt so good," Rayne answered.

"Good. That's what I like to hear. Now, how about some breakfast before you head on out to speak with Mark? Maybe you'd like a nice stack of flapjacks, some bacon and eggs and hot strong coffee?" Bessie said.

"Well, that sounds mighty fine."

Rayne allowed Bessie to lead her to a table in the corner. She looked at the woman. "I still can't believe they are gone."

"It'll take time."

Rayne sat waiting for her coffee and the mouthwatering meal that Bessie had described to her. She watched as the town's residents slowly entered the establishment. Mostly men, ranchers she imagined, ranchers who were just itching to take her uncle's land off her hands. Of course, there were some that looked at her with barely concealed lust in their eyes. If she been so inclined, some of the men she saw were handsome enough. What caught her attention was the fact that some of the people she noticed sneaking glances at her were attractive women.

Don't bother even imagining that, she told herself. *You brought enough troubles on yourself back in Boston. Besides, they are probably more curious about what I'm doing, or whether or not I have my sights set on their men.* She shivered at the thought of what they would think if they knew the truth.

Bessie placed a plate of food in front of her. "There you go. Enjoy."

"Thanks, it looks good." Rayne ate her food absently as her thoughts turned to the past.

Boston seemed so long ago, when in reality it had only been five months since she left her home and her family. The months had been hard and lonely. The only family members, including her immediate family, who understood her had been her Aunt Martha and Uncle Luke. They were the only ones who didn't turn their backs on her—the only ones that she knew of. It was hard to say what her two sisters and her brother thought. Her brother was probably still mad that she took his best clothing.

To be fair, her aunt and uncle were the only ones she even wanted to keep in touch with. She was scared to let her mother know where she was and had no clue about her father or if he was even still alive. She was sure the law was looking for her.

She reached up and put her hand over her cheek still feeling the sting of her father's hand. The events of that evening came back full force…

"You will marry Martin Sinclair in a week, girl, it's all been arranged."

"But, Father, I don't know him nor do I love him. His breath smells awful and I can't stand it when he touches me."

"You will grow to love him, child. He is a well-respected man in this community and he needs a wife. You are old enough to marry and he has promised to make you a decent husband."

"Father, please…"

"There will be no more said on the subject."

"Father, please don't make me do this," she had begged.

A hand struck her on the left side hard enough that she saw stars.

"Do not argue with me. You will do as I say without question."

She hadn't meant to kill her father but he sure had looked dead when she left the house that day. Now she was always on the run, worried that someone would show up and arrest her for murder.

"Rayne, sweetie…are you all right?" Bessie asked.

"Sorry, what did you say, Bessie?"

"I asked if there was anything more I could get you."

"Oh. No. I'm stuffed. Besides, I need to head out and find that lawyer fellow." Rayne stood.

"Are you all right there, young lady?" Bessie asked.

"Yeah, I'm fine. I was just remembering things," Rayne said.

"Hmm, well okay, if you say so. Look, I'm here if you ever want to just talk. Sometimes it just helps to talk, ya know."

"I know. Thanks."

"Well, you don't be a stranger, all right?"

"I won't. Thank you for the delicious meals and the heavenly bed. I will be back for more of that steak, that's for sure. How much do I owe you for all of it?" Rayne asked picking up her saddlebags.

"Well, I reckon four bits will cover it all."

"That's a mighty fair price for two meals and a soft bed," Rayne commented.

"Keeps my customers happy, and makes them want to stop back by on their way through town," Bessie responded with a smile and a wink

†

It appeared that the lanky man, dressed in a tailor-made suit, had just opened his office door and sat down for the day when Rayne walked in. He immediately looked up with a smile as he stood. "You must be Rayne Mathews. I'm Mark Benton. Let me welcome you to Willow Springs."

"Thank you. From what I've seen so far, it's a nice town and news sure travels fast." Rayne replied. "It is my understanding that my Uncle Luke left his place to me."

"Yes, he did. I've tried to keep it up since his passing."

"I appreciate that. Are there any papers I need to sign or anything? How much do I owe you?"

"None at all, on both counts. I sold the cattle that your uncle had and took my fee right off the top. The rest is in an account for you at the bank. I did ride out there yesterday and made sure there weren't any unwanted varmint of any variety stayin' out there. To be honest, the place looks good. There may be a few things that need fixin' up but nothing huge. I'm sure by the time winter comes, the Rocking M Ranch will look in fine shape."

"Thanks, I hope what you're sayin' is true. I can't wait to get out there and take inventory and see what needs to be done to it. " Rayne said.

"Well then, let's get you going. If you want, I'll ride out with you. First we can stop by the bank and introduce you to Tim Wilson. He runs the bank."

"That sounds great." Rayne nodded and headed out the door with the attorney close behind.

The introductions at the bank didn't take long. Wilson was a short, round man with a sour look on his face. Rayne shook his limp, sweaty hand then surreptitiously wiped her hand along her pants leg. "Nice to meet you, Mr. Wilson."

"I'm a very busy man, Miss Mathews. I'll get you

your bank book but know it isn't much." He looked squarely at Rayne. "You have no business doing a man's work. You should just sell the place and settle down somewhere else. With a husband."

Rayne's jaw worked as she suppressed anger toward the banker. "If I can just get my account information I'll be on my way."

"Very well, young lady, but mark my words you are making a big mistake."

In less than a minute, Wilson returned and shoved a small bankbook at her. "Is there anything else," he said brusquely.

"No." Rayne knew the instant she saw the amount in her account that it wouldn't last long. As soon as she was able, she would close the account, ride into the neighboring town, and find a banker who wasn't as rude as Tim Wilson was. *Hopefully there is one,* she thought. Rayne turned and left the bank quickly with the lawyer scurrying along behind her.

"Miss Mathews, wait a moment please," Mark Benton said.

Rayne turned around on the sidewalk and waited for the lawyer to catch up.

"I want you to know that not everyone in town is like Mr. Wilson."

"Yes, I understand. I'm just going to the livery to get my horse, then we can ride out to the place."

The lawyer nodded. "I'll meet you in front of my office then."

As the two rode out to her ranch, Mark filled Rayne in about the ranch and the town.

"You'll find most everyone in town is friendly and nice. I know some of them have been gossiping about you but they don't mean any harm. As for Mr. Wilson, I know he was a bit gruff with you but that's his way. Just steer clear of him and if he says anything to you, just smile. He is a very influential man and not someone you want to be on your wrong side.

"Thanks for the advice," Rayne said. "But you haven't changed my mind about the man. I know he is going to be trouble and I want to avoid trouble at all costs."

"Then don't rile him."

Perturbed, Rayne looked at the lawyer, ready to challenge him.

"Look up ahead on the right, Miss Matthews." The tall man pointed to where a fence began. "That's your place now."

The problem with the banker vanished from her mind that moment when she saw the land. Her land.

"Over there is the boundary that marks your land."

As they rode over the rise, they pulled their horses to a stop.

"There." The lawyer pointed down into the valley. "That's all yours."

Rayne looked down into a valley covered with lush green grass with a silver-tinged creek running through it.

"If you look closely," he pointed to a barely visible fence. "That's the fence that marks your property. Can you see the house there?"

Rayne nodded as she spied the house set just off from the creek next to a barn, and another building that looked like a small bunk house.

"Is that part of the boundary?" Rayne asked.

He nodded. "I'll ride the fence line with you and show you where the canyon is and where the end of your property is."

Rayne was in awe of what her uncle had left her. She was also a little overwhelmed with the responsibility that lay ahead of her in getting the ranch back into shape.

"Miss Mathews, there are a lot of people here that thought highly of your aunt and uncle. If there's anything you need, please don't hesitate to ask."

"Thank you, Mr. Benton."

"It's Mark. Please feel free to stop by for anything. Once you are settled, the wife would like you to come by for dinner. In fact, she told me to invite you this evening. May I tell her you'll be joining us?"

"That's a very kind offer. Considering I don't have any supplies here and I'm sick of biscuits and beans, I'd be happy to accept the offer."

"Great, I'll tell Emily to expect you around sundown?"

"That sounds great."

"Fantastic. Just ride to my office and we can go from there. All right?"

"You bet, and thank you for everything, Mark."

After riding the fence line the two rode back to the meadow where, what was now Rayne's new home, stood.

"Thank you for showing me the property, Mark. It's quite something. ."

"You're very welcome. Now, don't forget about dinner. I'll see you then."

Rayne watched as Mark headed back to town before she dismounted the big bay. She took her time and walked around the outside her new home taking inventory on what needed to be done. When she stepped into the house, her heart sank with the realization that never again would her aunt greet her with fresh baked cookies, nor would she smell the scent of her uncle's tobacco as he lit his pipe. While walking through the house she had to smile at long forgotten memories. She was touched anew by the sight of a special item that her aunt had loved and treasured. Bits and pieces of forgotten conversation filled her mind and made her heart soar. How she had loved them!

The house was small, for it had only been the two of them, but Luke and Martha Mathews had loved the place. The kitchen looked tidy and neat. While there was room for a new stove, she knew her Aunt Martha preferred saving the money and cooking out of the fireplace with the well-built hearth providing her with plenty of space.

Rayne turned around and walked back outside, and began walking around the grounds. Before she knew it, she stripped off her top shirt and was hard at work scooping out the rotted straw and hay in the barn before tearing off rotted boards. She looked out the barn window and judged by the sun that it was late afternoon. Rayne shook her head at all the work she wanted to do before heading to the creek to wash up and leave in time to meet Mark and his wife for dinner.

She stopped for a moment and leaned against the barn as her eyes surveyed the area. Her heart broke anew and sadness filled her mind. She had so looked forward to seeing them again, Becoming the owner of their place was nothing she had ever imagined would happen. Her Uncle Luke and Aunt Martha were gone and she would never see them again. She swiped at the tears that began as a single one rolling down her cheeks but turned into a sudden torrent that she could not stop.

✝

Dinner that evening was delightful. The meal was delicious and the company entertaining and friendly. Rayne enjoyed the time she spent with Mark and his wife, Emily, who she found to be an excellent cook.

"Emily, I must tell you how much I enjoyed this meal. The roast was perfectly cooked and moist." Rayne smiled at the woman. "I loved the carrots and the roasted potatoes were delicious. When I was growing up, we had a cook for about a year that made the best meals. After she left we never did have another cook who cooked as good. She has had no rival until tonight."

"Why, thank you, Rayne." Emily blushed.

The three talked and laughed until late that evening.

"Would you look at the time," Emily said finally. "Rayne it is much too late for you to ride home on an unfamiliar road. You might get lost. Please stay with us."

"I'll be okay and if I think need to stay over, I can get a room at Bessie's place."

"Nonsense. We have a perfectly good extra bedroom that you can use."

"I wouldn't want to put you out."

"You won't. Now I won't hear another word on the subject. You are staying here tonight."

"I insist that you stay, Rayne. Emily is right, it's much too late to have you out riding in the darkness trying to find your place," Mark said.

Rayne could see the love and devotion he held for his wife in his eyes and, deep in her heart, she felt a pang of envy.

"If you don't stay, I won't sleep a wink," Emily said.

"In that case, how can I not accept your invitation? I couldn't have you not sleeping because of me. If you're sure I'm not imposing." Rayne smiled at the smaller woman.

Emily beamed and soon Rayne found herself in the guest room.

Chapter Three

The fire was warm and crackling in the fireplace and the soft sound of the wind blew against the outside of the small house. She felt soft kisses and whispered words against her neck. She heard soft laughter and murmurs as she felt fingertips gently roaming over her naked body. The scent of roses drifted to her nose. Her heart raced and she felt as if she could not get enough of either air or of the tender touches. As she felt the warm mouth leave her lips, her eyes opened to see the golden blonde hair pushed back from the face that looked down at her.

She heard sharp knocking at the door and the woman vanished.

Rayne sat straight up in the bed and looked around as sweat rolled off her. "Oh, God. Not again,"' she whispered.

"Rayne." Emily's voice came through the door. "Coffee and breakfast are ready."

"Be right there," Rayne answered. Sanity and re-alization reclaimed her mind and with a low groan, she fell back against the pillow. *Who is she?* It wasn't the first dream she'd had of the woman. In each dream she would catch a glimpse of the woman only to wake in a sweat with her heart racing and an ache deep within. It was making her crazy.

"God, help me find this woman or put me out of my misery." Rayne whispered as she rose and dressed to face the day.

With a hug from Emily and a promise to return soon, Rayne headed toward town with Mark. She had a list of supplies that she had made the day before. Her plan was to stop by the mercantile, place an order, and buy a few items that she could take back with her. She also wanted to see if she could set up a delivery of lumber. Mark had given her a couple of leads on where she might be able to find a wagon, and a couple of horses, and the name of a rancher that had a few cattle he wanted to get rid of.

"I'm no rancher," Mark said. "But from what I could tell, the cattle looked in good shape."

"I'll have to look into them." Rayne knew quite a bit about livestock since, while traveling with the wagon train, Wilber Richardson had taught her how to size up cows and pick the ones that were the healthiest. As for horses, it was from her Uncle Luke that she had learned what to look for and recognize as a solid horse.

Once in town, Mark rode toward his small office and Rayne made her way to Gillum's mercantile. She dismounted and tethered Apache to the hitching post in front. As soon as she stepped up to the boardwalk, she heard a deep voice calling to her from across the street. She looked up to see Jeremiah Sprigs rapidly crossing to join her.

"Well, good morning to you, Miss Mathews. It's a fine day isn't it?" He gave Rayne a big smile.

"Mornin', Mr. Sprigs. Yes, it is a fine day."

"Oh, here, let me get that for ya." He rushed to open the door to the mercantile for her, and once she passed through, he stepped in behind her.

Rayne flashed Sprigs a smile that stopped short of her deep blue eyes. She headed to the counter, where the owner stood, or so she assumed. He was a short man with a trim body. "Hello, I'm Rayne Mathews. I'm lookin' for Mr. Gillum."

"Well that would be me, missy. What can I get fer ya?"

"To start off with, I'll need a couple of pounds of bacon, some flour, salt, pepper. Do you have any type of fresh meat?" Rayne asked.

"We got some fresh venison, elk, a few chickens…what would you like?"

"I suppose a couple of chickens and some elk, just what I can carry in saddle bags for now, but once I get a wagon I suppose I'll be wantin' more,"

"Miss Mathews, I can help ya out with some fresh beef if you'd like." Sprigs walked up behind Rayne. "I'd be happy to drop it by later, maybe you could cook up a couple of steaks, and we could get to know each other a bit better." He smiled at her.

Rayne's skin crawled. "I appreciate the offer, Mr. Sprigs, but I don't wanna put you out, nor do I want to cut you short on your own meat supply." Rayne looked at him and then back to Mr. Gillum. "I got a list here for the rest of the supplies I'll need. If you can get em ready for me, I'll be back in a couple of days to pick it all up."

"Now, missy, ya wouldn't be putting me out nor

cutting me short, after all, what are neighbors for? It would be my pleasure to help ya out, and I gotta say I'm kinda getting tired of my own cookin'. The company of a beautiful dinner companion and some stimulating conversation would be nice."

"Mr. Sprigs, I just moved into town and I'm tryin' to fix up my home and get settled. Entertaining a total stranger, let alone cooking for him, is not something I find appealing right now. I've tried to be polite today but you are not pickin' up on that. Thank you for your offer of the beef, but no thank you." Rayne turned and started to walk to the door.

"Mr. Gillum, thank you for your help. I'll be by in a couple of days to pick up the supplies and pay you for them."

"Welcome to town, Miss. Mathews." The owner behind the counter smiled as he looked up from the list Rayne handed him.

"Where do you think you're goin?" Sprigs' hand shot out and grabbed Rayne's arm. "You ain't gonna talk to me that way and just walk out."

Rayne's eyes flashed with anger and her tone was cold as ice when she looked up from the hand that had grabbed her arm into the eyes of its owner. "Let go of me now."

The short man behind the counter walked around toward Rayne and Sprigs.

Just then, the door of the store opened and the sheriff walked in. He seemed to size up the situation right away. "Sprigs, Cyrus, how are things goin'? Is there some trouble here?" the sheriff asked.

Sprig's hand dropped immediately. With a red face, he looked at the sheriff. "No. Nothing at all, Tom. All is fine. Cyrus, I forgot I got some things I need to do. I'll be back later with a list of things I need."

Sprigs rushed out of the shop.

"Looks like I walked into something here. Either of you wanna fill me in?" the tall sheriff asked.

"Old Jeremiah has a thick head, Tom. This here is Luke and Martha Mathews kin, Rayne. She stopped in to leave an order for supplies and well, Jeremiah decided since he was polite enough to offer some fresh meat to Miss Mathews, the least she could do was cook him dinner. The lady declined both offers and he didn't appreciate that."

Tom finally looked at Rayne and nodded. "Miss Mathews, welcome to Willow Springs. My condolences to you. Your Aunt Martha and Uncle Luke were fine people and we miss them. I wanna also apologize for Sprigs. He ain't got the manners God gave a goose. I don't believe he means any harm, he is just a might pushy at times." The sheriff offered his hand.

Rayne took his hand. "Sheriff, nice to meet you. I was gonna stop by your office later. I'd like to talk to you about Uncle Luke and Aunt Martha's death."

"All right. I'm not quite sure what I can tell you but if you're ready we can talk now." The big man said with a warm smile, and held the door open for Rayne.

Together Rayne and the sheriff walked toward his office.

Chapter Four

For the past ten years, Tom Kennedy had lived in Willow Springs and had been sheriff for the past six years. He liked his job and cared about most of the people in Willow Springs. With the exception of a few rabble-rousers, the town was quiet and peaceful. Like any town of course, it had its share of troublemakers and youngsters looking for trouble. Also, an occasional cowboy would get out of hand when he got to drinking or thought someone had cheated at cards. Overall though, he had nothing bad to say about his town.

Jeremiah Sprigs, on the other hand, was a completely different matter. Tom wasn't sure there was anything truly good he could say about the man. In his opinion, the man was a lying sleazebag. He treated women badly, and his animals even worse—the ones he worked with anyway—the others, like the cattle he sold, were well-fed and healthy animals. That was the best Tom could say about the man.

After they entered the Sheriff's office, Tom closed the door behind them.

"Please, Miss Mathews, take a seat."

Rayne sat in a sturdy wooden chair. "Thank you for taking time to speak with me, Sheriff."

"Always glad to oblige." The sheriff sat behind his desk and gave Rayne a stern look. "I hope you don't take Jeremiah Sprigs to be the best example of the folks around these parts. Most are very kind and caring of their neighbors," the sheriff said.

"My name is Rayne and I'd appreciate it kindly if you called me that."

Rayne smiled.

"As for Sprigs, no, I don't hold him as any example of folks around here. I met Bessie last night, and like you, she assured me that he is the lowest life form around."

With a deep laugh, Tom shook his head. "That sounds like something Bessie would say."

He looked at Rayne. She was tall for a woman, had long black hair and a pleasant face. He suspected that many of the bachelors in town would try to court her. Somehow, he didn't think that was what she wanted. "So, Rayne, what can I tell you about your Aunt and Uncle?"

"I don't know. I guess there's no way to know if they suffered, or…"

"Rayne, Luke and Martha… they was good people. I'm sorry to say there isn't any way to tell just how long they laid out there in pain or if it was quick. They didn't even have anyone to send for the doc."

The sheriff looked at Rayne as he gauged what to say next.

"Whose land borders mine?" Rayne asked, as if reading his mind.

"I'm sad to say, Sprigs is your neighbor on three sides of ya. His land takes up a little past the creek."

"Oh, that's downright nice. I supposed I should

expect to see him often then." She frowned.

"Look, I won't say ya got nothing to worry about as far as he goes, cuz word is he would love to have that land of yours. But I don't believe that he would do anything to harm you…or your kin folk…in order to get it," the sheriff stated. "Is that what you're worried about?"

"I guess that was some of my concern. Thanks, Sheriff. I suppose I should head on back to the place. I've got a lot of work ahead of me." She put her hands on her knees ready to stand.

"Was that all you wanted to know? I mean, I kinda got the feeling that you had something specific in mind. I don't see how I could have answered anything," Tom said.

"Sheriff, I was just…oh hell, I don't know. Just seems like Uncle Luke and Aunt Martha were fine one day and gone the next. In the last letter I got from Uncle Luke some time ago, he mentioned some troubles he was having, but he didn't go into detail. Did he ever come and talk to you about anything?"

"No, he never stopped by or said anything to me."

Tom thought about the last time he had seen Luke Mathews. It had been about a week before the illness took them. He remembered that at the time, Luke seemed to have something on his mind. It was nothing he wanted to talk about and Tom was in a hurry so he didn't push the man. Now, he was wishing he had. He meant to ask him about it the next time he'd seen him unfortunately the chance never came. He was escorting a prisoner to a neighboring town when the deaths happened. When he returned, he heard the sad news.

"Rayne did your Uncle give you any idea of what was going on? Now that I think of it, he was acting kind of strange the last time I saw him. I meant to ask him about it but I'm sad to say that never happened."

"No, he didn't. He just wrote that he was having some troubles. It was nothing specific."

"Okay. If you think or remember anything, let me know. In the meantime I'll see if I can find anything out from the folks in town."

"I'll think about it and see if I can remember, but I'm thinking that was the only time he ever mentioned any trouble." Rayne stood, nodded at the sheriff, and held out her hand. "Sheriff, thank you for your time."

Tom took Rayne's hand and shook it. "I am always available. If you can't find me just ask one of my deputies and they'll know where I am."

"I'll remember that, Sheriff."

"I'd be pleased if you'd call me Tom. That's what most folks call me."

Rayne smiled. "Thank you, Tom."

Tom watched as Rayne left his office and made her way across the street to her horse. From what he could tell, she would be a nice addition to his town.

†

The eyes watching from across the street were cold and held rage. *How dare she speak to me the way she did. Once I'm married to her, I'll have to teach her exactly how to speak to a man.* The thought played in Sprigs' mind of all the ways he would teach the dark haired woman to obey him. Some thoughts brought a little thrill as he could almost feel the pain radiate from the woman's body, while other thoughts made his groin tighten a bit.

"Oh, yeah, Miss Mathews, you're gonna learn how to respect a man."

He let out a cold laugh as he watched her mount her horse.

Chapter Five

The weeks flew by as Rayne either worked on her place or went into town for more lumber and nails. The first thing she did was buy a wagon and two horses. Once that was done, Rayne picked up her order from Gillum's Mercantile and headed to her place to start working on repairs.

Now, as she surveyed the place, she realized that she had pretty much finished all the hardest work. Rayne stood with her arms resting on a shovel and looked at what she accomplished thus far. The outbuildings were complete and the fencing around the barn done. She had the blisters to prove that she split all the rails by hand, but damn, she felt good. She smiled fondly as she recalled all the times she pestered her uncle into letting her help him around the place. He taught her the proper respect for the land along with how to swing a hammer and cut a board.

This was her place. She was pouring her heart, blood, sweat, and tears into it and she was damned proud of that fact. With the barn and the fencing done, she could now start on her herd. By her count, she still had close to seven hundred dollars in hard cash in the bank so that should get her well on the way to a great start.

"Yup, we're looking damn good here, Apache.

Don'tcha think?"

The big bay standing next to her was grazing on a patch of luscious green grass. He gave her a soft snort and lifted his head slightly before going back to eating. Her eyes rested on the two younger horses that she had recently bought. She had named them Samson and Delilah because the moment she saw the mare the name Delilah had popped into her head.

"What do you think, Samson?" She rubbed the velvet nose of the horse. "You feelin' up to headin' into Sulfur Springs and seein' if we can get a few head of cattle? Think you're up for a cattle drive?"

The horse neighed.

So far, the only thing Rayne had used the two horses for since coming to her ranch was to pull the wagon to and from town loaded with supplies, lumber, and grain.

"Tomorrow morning we'll head out, stop in town and set Apache and Delilah up either at the livery stable or maybe over at Mark's place," she said as she continued to stroke the bay's nose before giving him and the other two horses pieces of carrot. "We'll have to see if he's up to watchin' over you two while I'm gone."

With plans made, Rayne led the three horses into their respective stalls inside the barn. She gave each a bucket of oats before heading in to take care of her own meal.

As she walked toward her house, she looked at the setting sun and the beauty of the land that lay in front of her. A feeling of calm fell upon her. "This is what it's all about. God, this is beautiful."

With a final look, she went inside and started dinner.

†

The next morning, Rayne rose early and headed out to the barn to saddle Sampson. While working at her task she spoke to Delilah and Apache. "Okay, here's the plan. Ol' Samson here is gonna go with me and you and Delilah are gonna stay in town. There's no way I can ride three horses and drive cattle so ya both will stay in town and not cause trouble, ya hear. I'm thinkin' Lucifer will be goin' with us as well. He can keep the cattle in line."

She looked over at the big black dog who sat staring at her. The dog had appeared one night and just made himself at home. She had no idea if the animal was good with cattle or not but at this point, she had to try something since it was about time the dog did something to earn his keep. She really had no idea why she named the animal Lucifer other than when he bared his teeth and growled, it sounded like the devil himself had been unleashed.

That's exactly what the dog had done when she unexpectedly happened upon a rattler sunning on a rock. The rattle on his tail started shaking and the snake looked like it was about to strike when the dog appeared at her side, baring teeth and growling fiercely. Before she could react, the dog had lunged at the snake and caught its neck between his teeth. Up until that point, the only thing Rayne had called the animal was *dog*. At that moment, the only thought in her head was that the dog looked like Lucifer himself waging war on some unsuspecting creature. The minute she thought that, the dog looked at her as he licked his lips and the look in his eyes was one that had reminded Rayne of the devil. Luckily for her, the dog seemed to like her and had never showed her that side of him since that day—she never encouraged him to either.

Together, the dog, three horses, and their owner set off toward town. True to her word, she rode up to Marks office, tethered the horses to the hitch, and told Lucifer to sit while she went in to speak to Mark. When she came out, Mark was with her and Lucifer let out a low growl.

"Lucifer, *no*. He's a friend." Rayne's voice was firm and Lucifer backed off.

They walked toward Mark's home with the three horses in tow, making their way to the barn behind his house.

"Thanks, Mark I really appreciate your helpin' me out like this."

She mounted Samson and looked down at her friend. "I'll be back as soon as I can."

She rode away with the dog trotting behind her.

Rayne's next stop before leaving town was the bank where she once again had to deal with the unpleasant banker, Timothy Wilson. His manner was condescending and bordering on rude where Rayne was concerned. He acted as if giving Rayne *her* money was robbing his own pocket when in fact the money was hers, not his

"Miss Mathews, I think you're making a big mistake thinking you can manage a ranch. Why don't you let me make some inquires. I know quite a few men who would be interested in taking the place off your hands. As far as a withdrawal, I believe the best thing to do is leave your money and the account alone."

"Mr. Wilson, thank you for your concern over my account but I assure you I am very capable of managing my own affairs. And since it seems so very hard for you to understand that, I do believe I'll be closing this account."

"I don't believe that would be wise nor do I believe that is what Mr. Benton would want."

"First off, you have no right to decide for me what is wise or not. Mr. Benton is not my father nor is he my husband. He did what he thought was best at the time when he sold my uncle's cattle and placed the money in an account in my name. Mr. Wilson, the account *is* in my name and therefore I can do anything I please with it. So now, if you would kindly bring me the money that this statement…" She held up the piece of paper he'd given her when she arrived. "…says is in my account I'll be taking it with me and closing this account."

Yet he persisted. "Now, Miss Mathews, I don't think that would be the smart thing to do."

"Mr. Wilson, is there anyone else listed on the account?"

"Why, no there isn't."

"As far as you know, *I* am Rayne Mathews, the owner of the account in question? Have I provided papers and letters as proof that I am who I claim to be?"

"Well, yes…but…"

"No buts about it. I want all seven hundred dollars that this bankbook says is mine and I want it now. Otherwise, I suppose we can both take a walk over to Sheriff Kennedy's office and talk to him about it,"

"Oh, very well, Miss Mathews, I'll be right back." The balding, fat man's face burned red with fury. In a few minutes, he returned with two stacks of bills and a paper for her to sign. She had him count out the bills to make sure there was the exact amount, not a cent less or a cent more than what was due her. And once she was satisfied, she signed the paper, placed the money in her saddlebags, and walked out of the bank, hoping and praying she would never have to deal with the man again.

With the saddlebag secured to her saddle, she mounted and headed out of town.

Rayne had a smile on her face for the way she had stood up to the obnoxious banker. She had grown from a subservient daughter to a confident woman. She had been so preoccupied about getting away from her home in Boston and keeping out of the law's way that she forgot about her birthday three months before. So far, no one had treated her like a seventeen-year-old child and she was pleased that no one realized just how young she was.

That night found her, Lucifer, and Samson under the stars next to a nice warm campfire. As she thought and gazed at the stars, it occurred to her that she was finally home. In fact, the only area where she felt any dissatisfaction was that she was alone. She had no one to come home to after she finished her chores, and no one to share her life. It was the companionship of couples and families that she missed so much. At times, it made her hurt. When she saw her new friends, Mark and Emily, and all the love and closeness radiating from them, she felt lost. It was the one point of running away from Boston that made her sad.

"This is the life you chose, Rayne," the little voice in her head said.

"Well, yeah, but damn, at times it's lonely." She answered herself as she closed her eyes and drifted to sleep. Again, she dreamt of a little blonde woman with blue eyes.

With the rising sun, Rayne was ready to finish her ride to the small town of Cherokee Falls. Armed with money and a couple of names, she was ready to fulfill her dream for the ranch. By mid morning, she had arrived and, with a few questions, she was able to locate Joel Matters and Abel West.

"What can I do for you little lady?" Joel Matters asked.

"I'd like to see about buyin' a few head of cattle from you."

"How many you thinkin' about?" Abel West asked.

"If your cattle are as good as I hear, I'm lookin' to buy around thirty head."

"We can handle that. Why don't you git off your

horse and follow me to the corral," Matters said.

With both men in the lead, Rayne followed them to the corral that was located behind the barn.

"These here are ones we were fixin' to sell. As you can see, they are fat and happy."

Rayne went inside the corral and, running her hands over each one, she noted they all looked healthy and free from disease. "How much?"

West ran his hand over his face. "Now, these here are prime beef cattle and we would probably be sellin' them for...." He looked at his partner. "Three dollars and two bits."

"That there is the lowest price you'll find around these parts," Matters added.

Rayne calculated it would cost her almost a hundred dollars. She walked back among the cows and looked them over again.

"Do you have any milk cows?"

"We can sell you one for the same price," West said,

Rayne nodded. She suddenly realized the enormity of driving thirty cows along. "I have a place outside of Willow Springs, how much to have you drive them there?"

"What's your name, little lady?" Matters was studying her.

"Rayne Mathews."

"Hell, why didn't you say that from the beginnin', girl. I know'd your uncle Luke ever since he started ranchin'. I sold him his first cattle. Sure a shame what happened to him and the missus." He took his hat off and with his sleeve wiped the sweat off his forehead. "Tell you what I'm gonna do for you. You can have the thirty head, the milk cow, a young bull, and we'll drive em to your place for a hundred and twenty."

"That sounds good to me." Rayne held out her hand and shook each man's hand. "Thank you." She reached into her saddlebags, counted out the money, and handed it to West.

"Thank you kindly." West tipped his hat.

"We should have the cattle to you by the end of the week," Matters said.

"I'm much obliged." Rayne put her foot in a stirrup and swung her other leg over Samson. "See you then."

With a smile, Rayne headed to the bank with what was left of her money. She hoped that the banker there wasn't a complete ass like Timothy Wilson who apparently held women in low regard.

As she walked into the Cherokee Falls Bank, she was greeted by a dark haired man dressed in a well-made suit. He stood immediately and flashed a welcoming smile at her.

"Welcome, I'm Jefferson Smith. How can I help you?" he asked as he held out his hand.

"Hello. I'm Rayne Mathews and I'd like to see about opening an account here." She accepted the outstretched hand.

"Of course, Miss Mathews. I'd be glad to set you up with an account."

The man pulled out papers and began the process of opening an account for Rayne. Within an hour,

Rayne had a new account that held the remainder of her money.

With a huge smile and a satisfied feeling, Rayne once again mounted her horse and headed for the town hotel in search of a good meal before she returned back home. She debated about getting a room. It was already mid-afternoon and the ride back was long. If she left now, she was looking at riding all night just to get back to her ranch. As she rode down the main street of the town, she saw a couple of saloons and licked her parched lips. A drink would be a nice treat.

Chapter Six

Rayne gently tugged the reins to the right and guided Samson toward a hitching post. After dismounting, and telling Lucifer to stay put, Rayne pushed through swinging doors leading inside the saloon. The chatter stopped and all eyes turned to her. Rayne could see the shock in some of the eyes. They challenged her right to enter their establishment while others were just looking to see who had come in. As she walked toward the long bar, she noticed some of the working girls flashing her big smiles, She returned the smiles. Once at the bar she took up a spot and immediately ordered a draft. The bartender pulled back on the tap, filled a glass of beer, and slid it down the bar to her before waiting on other customers. She took a long drink and felt the cold refreshing liquid flow down her throat.

"God, that's good," she gasped

"Sure does hit the spot, doesn't it?" The man standing next to her on the right had silver gray hair and looked to be about sixty years old.

Rayne grinned. It was far from normal for any man talk to her in a bar. Usually, if they did, it was to tell her to go home where she belonged. Thrown by the man's comment, she looked around to see if he had been speaking to someone else.

The man smiled at her. "Ain't talkin' to no one but you, stranger. Most around here are either too drunk to hold a conversation or just wanna take my money. So I don't bother. You, on the other hand, just came in so you gotta be sober and ya appreciate a nice cool beer. It occurred to me that you might be good at conversation, so thought I'd agree with ya. Now, can ya converse or just stand there with that silly look on yer face?" The man took a swig of his beer.

"I suppose I can converse, used to be able to, at any rate. Been a while since I was put on the spot though so I might be a mite rusty at it so don't go holdin' it against me, all right?"

"Well, all righty then. I won't hold that against ya at all, hell, only one I talk to most times is Scruffy my dog and well, he ain't all that good at it. He mostly just wants his food. Ya know?"

"Totally understand, old Lucifer is pert near the same way…course I talk to him and he looks at me like I gone and lost my mind. Not Apache though, he understands me."

"Now who is Apache?"

"That would be the big bay that's hitched out at a friend's barn back home."

"Ah, okay, yeah. I use to talk to Apollo before I met my wife." He laughed. "The funny thing is, she sort of took offense when I talked to the horse instead of her. Can you imagine that? So to keep peace in the house, I gave up telling all my secrets to old Apollo. I'm thinkin' that he got brokenhearted 'cause he was never quite the same after I got the missus."

"Oh, really? I suppose I can see where Apollo woulda got his feelin's hurt." Rayne gave the man a serious look but had amusement in her voice.

"Let me get ya another beer. Jacob, get us two more, all right?" the man said. "I'm Martin by the way. Nice to meet ya,"

"Nice to meet you too. I'm Rayne." Rayne put her hand out to Martin.

"So what brings you to Cherokee Falls?"

"Well, I came to buy a few head of cattle from Joel Matters and Abel West."

"Oh, I hope you succeeded. They both have some mighty fine looking herds."

"I managed to get a few. They will drive them to my ranch by week's end." Rayne heard a touch of pride in her voice.

"So, I take it since you're having them driven to your place that you ain't livin' here in Cherokee Falls."

"Nope, I got me a small ranch over in Willow Springs that I inherited from my uncle."

"Hell, you ain't kin to Luke and Martha Mathews are ya? Sorry about their passin', they was damn good people."

"Wait. You knew my Aunt and Uncle? Did you see them often? Were you good friends?" Rayne asked.

"Now hold on there, Sprout, let's get us a table and I'll tell you all you wanna know." The man headed for a table with his, and Rayne's, beer in hand.

Rayne followed the man and sat down. "How did

you know Uncle Luke?"

"Well, Luke and me rode here from Boston way back when. See, he was my best friend and neither of us wanted to go into our family's businesses. Now I ask ya, can you see Luke as a pompous preacher?"

Rayne shook her head.

"Nope, not me either. Hell, I couldn't see me behind some counter sellin' clothes to uppity people. So one day we just up and left. Figured on headin' to Montana, but we stopped here for supplies. Old Luke met your Aunt Martha and swore he wasn't leavin', so I decided I'd stick around long enough to see him settled with Martha. Hell, wouldn't ya know I got stuck for the winter and met my wife Sarah."

"Now that makes sense. Least now I understand why my father was always so...."

"Yeah, it would. Your pa, being the younger of the two, always dreamed of heading off and seekin' his own fortune. He counted on your uncle being the one stuck following his daddy's shoes…instead, it was him. Course it served the pompous ass right."

Martin shook his head. "Sorry, I know he's your pa and al, but he was a jackass when I knew him and I'm sure he ain't changed none."

"I..."

"You ain't spoke to your kin in a while, have you?"

"No, sir, I haven't. We kinda had a fallin' out, you could say."

"I ain't sure what happened, but your uncle did a get a letter telling him he should let 'em all know if he heard from you and if ya ever showed up. Luke was to send word so they could come get ya. If I remember correctly, he told me that he had sent word for 'em to go straight to hell. Said if you ran off it had to be cuz they done something really bad to ya."

"Can you remember who sent for me?" Rayne's eyes widened. *If I killed my father wouldn't the law come after me?*

"It was a letter from your pa. Single page near as I recall. It really made Luke mad. Not sure what it was all about but I gotta figure it was bad cuz ain't never seen Luke that mad before. Hell, he said after that he didn't have a brother. Maybe one day you'll feel comfortable enough with me to tell me what happened. I know you don't know me from Adam, but I loved your uncle like he was my own kin and I sorta feel like I…I don't know what I feel like. I owe it to him to watch out for you."

Rayne was at a loss as to what to say to that. Just as she was about to speak, the man began to speak again.

"Hey, look, I'm sorry I made ya uncomfortable. I was just…hell, I don't know. Luke was like my brother and you being his kin and all…damn I can't believe how much you resemble him. I hadn't noticed it before."

"Thank you." Rayne blushed. "So, uh, Martin, when was the last time you saw my uncle?"

"Oh, I suppose it was about a month or so before I heard about his passin'. Why you ask, youngun?"

"Did he mention to you any problems he was having with the ranch or anything like that?"

"Can't say that I recall. You sticking around or heading back to Willow Springs tonight?"

"I was thinkin' I'd get me a room, stay over, and head back come first light," Rayne answered.

"Why don't you come on home with me and have dinner with the missus and me. I'll see what I can recall and maybe Sarah might remember something too."

"Your wife won't mind at all?"

"Nope. She will be thrilled that I brought Luke's niece home."

"All right. Just let me get me a room first." Rayne got up to head to the hotel.

"Now hold on there, Sprout. Ain't no way I'm lettin' you take some room in town when I got a perfectly good room out at our place. 'Sides, the wife would have a fit. So you might as well plan on stayin' with me and the missus."

Martin pushed back his chair and stood. The decision was made.

Chapter Seven

Sprigs stormed into the bar madder than a bear with a thorn stuck in his paw. "Bring me a goddamn beer," he growled.

The barkeep Hank quickly went about grabbing a mug and placing the drink in front of the red-faced man. Hank turned away and rushed off to the other side of the bar to wait on another customer.

"Where the hell is that whore Fern?" Sprigs shouted.

The mood of the saloon changed and Sprigs felt a sense of power. He saw some, not many, grinning, and he knew why. They knew what was in store for the whore once he took her upstairs. The rest seemed to cower and he snarled at them. He knew they disapproved of him but he didn't care. A whore was a whore and he knew which one he wanted.

"Who do you think you're lookin' at," Sprigs growled. "Hell, most all of you use the women then go home to your wives. None of you would ever consider marrying a whore so don't look at me in disapproval. You're no better than me."

The saloon fell quiet.

"Hank, where in the hell are you and why ain't you answering me?" Sprigs bellowed.

"Calm down, Sprigs. I'm right here and I heard ya

the first damn time. Fern is upstairs, so either wait your turn or pick someone else. Looks like Elsie is free."

"Elsie. You gotta be kiddin' me. Elsie sure as hell ain't even close to something I want. She is mousy and skinny as shit and ain't got anything for a man to grab on to."

"Then wait your damn turn." Hank walked away to serve a cowboy at the end of the bar.

Sprigs, annoyed at having to wait, muttered and spewed his dislike of the situation. He narrowed his eyes. "Now wait a damn minute here, I pay good money for...."

Hank was beside him with an angry glare before Sprigs could finish his sentence. "No, Jeremiah, you wait a damn minute. You pay for what you buy, good or not, and your money ain't any better than anyone else's here. Now, I suggest you either buy another drink, go play cards and relax or get the hell out of here." Hank's jaw was set firmly.

Sprigs, who had been shocked that anyone would speak to him the way that bitch Mathews had a week ago, was even more shocked that Hank would speak to him the way he just had.

What the hell is goin on, who the hell do these people think they are?

He frowned, remembering the eyes he felt on him when he walked down the streets after that incident with the Mathews woman. He knew they were talking about how that woman dared to speak to him. He let the anger build in him and felt its power. *No matter, they'll be sorry, especially that bitch.*

"Fine, get me another beer and take it to my table and be sure to send Fern to me when she is done," he grumbled. All things considered he knew that today wasn't the day to start trouble.

Hank looked at the man and turned on his heel. After he drew another beer, he handed it to a younger barkeep who delivered it to Sprigs' table.

After three more drinks, a woman showed up at Sprigs' table with a ready smile on her lips as a hand slid over his shoulders. The soft, gentle fingers seemed to burn through the fabric of his shirt.

"Heard you been waitin' for me, handsome," Fern purred in a low sexy voice.

"Yup, what the hell took you so damn long?"

"Aw, you ain't the only man I see, baby." She slid onto his lap and smiled at him.

"Hmm, I'm the only one that counts though." He stood, dumping Fern out of his lap. His hand gripped her arm tight as he made his way toward the stairs, pulling her along with him.

Sprigs pulled her behind him toward the door of her room, which was in the far corner, right above the piano. Sprig realized, for the first time, that having this room meant no one would hear real screams. Sprigs was usually rough with Fern but he knew she didn't mind. His mood was particularly foul this time, thanks to the Mathews bitch, and he noticed that she trembled when she saw the look in his eyes. When Sprigs threw her on the bed and ripped at her clothes he knew she was scared and she actually let out a small scream. He reveled in her fear even as he slapped her across the face.

"Shut the hell up or you'll be sorry," he growled.

An hour and a half later, Sprig walked down the stairs and went straight to the bar where he ordered a whiskey. He downed it in one gulp. He tossed enough money on the bar to cover his afternoon, walked out to his horse, mounted it, and headed home. His anger over Rayne Mathews was still coursing through him.

"Goddamn bitch, wonder how she'd like a surprise visit in the middle of the night." The corner of his upper lip curled. "I think I just might do that."

This decision made, the rest of his ride home, he was in a much better mood.

The rest of the afternoon and evening flew by and soon Sprigs was back on his horse heading toward his neighbor's spread. He waited for the bitch to settle in for the night. Not seeing any light coming from the house, he began his way to sneak inside to teach her some manners. As he approached the little house, he noticed that indeed the lights were out, but something didn't feel right. It was too quiet, the air didn't smell right.

"Damn it, wish to hell there was some moon light." As he crept around, he realized that no animals were in the stables and what he had missed was smelling the smoke from the fireplace. The house was empty.

"Where the hell did she go? Goddamn it!" he shouted into the night.

Chapter Eight

Rayne enjoyed meeting her aunt and uncle's best friends. She was pleased finally to get to know her relatives through someone who had actually had contact with them in their later years. Yes, she had received letters from them but that really wasn't the same. She wanted to know the people they had become in the years after she had grown and stopped spending summers with them.

She found Martin and Sarah to be kind, friendly, and eager to share their memories of her Aunt Martha and Uncle Luke. She realized, through talking to the couple, that she missed her aunt and uncle more than she had thought. When Rayne asked Martin again if her uncle had any trouble before he died, the look that passed through his eyes was one of worry and regret.

"Yep, I do remember Luke mentioning some trouble the last time I seen him. Not that he went into detail, just that he'd noticed some tracks and some fences that had been messed with," Martin told her.

"Did he mention who he thought might be behind it?"

"Nope. If he suspected anyone, he didn't tell me." He eyed Rayne. "Child, what are you thinkin'?"

"Just…heck, I don't know. From what the sheriff tells me, it was an accident of fate that took 'em. I just can't help but feel there was somethin' else goin' on too."

"Well, I think you should just leave it all alone and concentrate on the here and now," Sarah said. "How about another piece of pie and some more coffee?"

"Oh, no thank you, I am stuffed." Rayne said with a smile. "Dinner was fantastic. I don't think I've ever had quail that tasted so good."

"Well thank you. Here, let me get that for you. Would you like to see your room? I'm sure you're tired. Martin will talk your ear off all night if I'd let him."

"Thank you, ma'am. I am plumb tuckered. I guess too much excitement today." Rayne realized that her eyes were slowly drooping and that weariness was settling in her shoulders. She was indeed done in.

Sarah showed Rayne to the guestroom and left her to relax.

†

"Do you think you did the right thing in telling her about Luke's suspicions?" Sarah asked her husband later when she walked back into the kitchen.

"The child has a right to know what she might be lookin' at. I mean, hell, she could start havin' the same troubles and a little warning might be helpful," Martin answered.

"Yes, but then again, she just might go lookin' for

that trouble. She seems to be too much like Luke and she even looks just like him. I'm worried about her,"

"We'll just have to keep an eye on her, honey."

"That's a little hard to do when she is a day's ride from here," Sarah countered.

"I'll take a ride in and have a talk with the sheriff."

"Martin, the sheriff's a busy man. He ain't gonna have the time to keep an eye on her."

"I know that, woman. At least he can stop by now and then and check on her. Now relax, we'll take care of that youngun, don't you worry," Martin said.

Chapter Nine

"Has anyone seen Fern?" Hank asked the young man who was behind the bar.

"Not that I know of. Last I seen of her was when she went up with Sprigs. Ask one of the other girls, I'm sure they'll know where she is."

"You're sure a lot of goddamn help," Hank muttered.

After asking everyone, he headed upstairs to the room the woman used. After knocking several times and getting no response, he opened the door to find the woman lying on the bed in a pool of blood.

He rushed over to the bed put his ear to her chest to listen for a heartbeat and found a very weak one. He ran out the door and to the head of the stairway where he stopped one of the women heading back down. "Run and get Doc Adams and then the sheriff."

Within minutes, the doctor arrived, soon followed by Sheriff Kennedy. The doctor looked Fern over and did what he could to make the woman comfortable.

"Only time will tell whether she'll pull through or not," he told the sheriff

"When was the last time you seen Fern, Hank?" Sheriff Kennedy asked.

"Saw her go up with Sprigs and don't recall seeing her after he had gone." He shrugged. "Although I can't swear to it."

After questioning Hank, Kennedy rode out to Sprigs' place. Once he got there he went to the main house and found no one there. Deciding to take a walk over to the bunk house, he spoke with a couple of the Sprig's cowboys and found out that Sprigs was in a foul mood when he rode out that morning and in a much better one when he returned. Most of the men said that as far as they knew Sprigs was up at the main house.

"You say Jeremiah was in a foul mood, any idea what that was about?" the sheriff asked

"Hell, with him you can never be sure, though it's my guess he was still pissed over the way that Mathews' gal spoke to him. I think he's got a hankerin' to taste that, and she ain't givin' him the time of day." Otis Wheatley, a lanky cowboy leaned against the wall as he waited for the others to back him up.

"Yup that's my guess. Hell, he should be up at the main house, why don't you go ask him, you're interruptin' our card game here." The grizzled man who spoke had a cigar hanging out of one corner of his mouth.

"Well he isn't there," the sheriff complained. "When you all see him, tell him I got a couple of questions for him. All right?" Once he saw at least one of the ranch hands nod, he tapped his horse's side and rode back toward town. As he rode, his mind was on Fern.

How am I going to proceed? I hope and pray that

the woman lives to tell me exactly what happened. If she dies, there isn't a damned thing I can do to Sprigs.

✝

Early the next morning Rayne said good-bye to her new friends, Martin and Sarah, after she saddled her horse. With one last goodbye, Rayne headed back to Willow Springs with Lucifer trotting beside her. She couldn't wait to get back and gather up Apache and Delilah and head home.

The ride was nice and quiet, and she did a lot of day dreaming and planning. *Yup my life is finally on the track I want,* she thought to herself. Aside from being alone, she was happy. The previous night she had once again dreamt about the blonde haired blue-eyed mystery woman and woke this morning with a sense of excitement she couldn't explain.

The dream had been so vivid she swore she could feel the woman in her arms and she awoke feeling warm and happy, filled with a love that she had never felt before in her life. The joy she felt in her dream transcended through to her waking state and that alone gave her hope.

"Samson, what do you think? You believe she is real and out there waitin' for me?" she asked. The big horse neighed and nodded his head, which caused her to smile. "Well all right then, if you think so, then it will all turn out as it should," she said with a laugh.

Chapter Ten

"So what you're tellin' me, Sprigs, is that it wasn't you that left Fern beaten and near death," the sheriff asked.

"She's a whore. Who cares what happens to her?" Sprigs replied.

"I do. If she dies, it's murder."

"Not me, Sheriff," Sprigs sneered. "Fern likes it rough and begs to be hit. If she is askin' for it and someone gives it to her, the blame is on her 'cause that is how she wanted it."

Sheriff Kennedy listened to the man's words. Words that almost admitted he'd beaten Fern up. "So were you the one who gave her what she wanted?"

"Yeah, I hit her a few times when she asked me to. As far as I'm concerned, she's a whore and that is what I pay her to be. There's no crime in that is there?"

"Yes, there is. If she dies you'll be the first one I come lookin' for." The sheriff's face was a deep red.

"Go ahead and try blamin' me for what some whore asked for. Unless you have any more accusations, I'm leaving." Sprigs rose and left the office.

†

The news wasn't good at Hank's bar, Fern was messed up bad and it didn't look like she was going to get any better. She hadn't regained consciousness and with each passing hour she was getting weaker. If one was to believe Doc Adams, it was only a matter of time before the woman passed on.

This news and the cost of the doc left Hank in a bad mood and in a bad position. He couldn't help Fern and he certainly couldn't afford one of his most popular girls being gone from the saloon. Facing the issue, he knew he'd have to put Emma out. Even though he knew it wasn't what Fern would have wanted.

"Look, with Fern gone, I'm losin' money, and it's about damn time you start earnin' your keep," he told Emma that evening after stopping her in the hallway. "Now tonight, I want you to wear a pretty dress and start serving the men their drinks. You work the floor, let 'em know you're there and soon enough someone will take interest in ya." Hank looked at the small blonde woman. She stood silently staring at the floor, tears in her eyes.

The other women gathered around Hank all in an uproar. One stood forward. "Hank, don't do that to her! Look, the rest of us will chip in a few dollars to help make up for what you're losin' for Fern."

"Mattie, keep outta this. It ain't up to you. My decision is final. Emma will start as a barmaid then work upstairs with you all. By this time next week, she should be earnin' Fern's share of the customers."

"Hank, please, I can't... I can cook and clean like I been doing but please don't make me...." Emma began.

Hank's hand across her cheek silenced her.

The women who worked the bar rushed to Emma and helped her up.

"Don't say anything," whispered Joan, one of the older working girls.

Emma held a hand to her cheek and said nothing more.

Hank, embarrassed by his actions but satisfied that he wouldn't get anymore back talk from his girls, walked along the hallway and down the stairs.. He liked Emma but he knew having fewer girls would lose him money and he had no choice. Emma would just have to do as he said.

Walking down the stairs, Hank spied Sprigs—the last person he wanted to see.

†

"Hank, how ya doin'?" Sprigs greeted the bar-keep. "I hear Fern is not doing too good. How is she?"

"Well, Sprigs, how do you think she is?" Hank answered calmly.

"If I knew, I wouldn't ask."

"She probably isn't going to make it."

"Well, shit. I'm sure sorry to hear that. She was…well, she was fun…what can I say? I suppose you'll be getting a new girl to replace her. You be sure to let me know when ya do. I just might be interested, if ya know what I mean."

Deep inside Sprigs was glad to hear that the whore was going to die. Without her testimony no one could say it was him that done the deed.

"Jesus, Sprigs, the woman ain't even cold yet." Hank shook his head sadly.

"Well, maybe not but you be sure to let me know." Sprigs walked off to the bar where he ordered a shot of whiskey.

God, I hope whoever that asshole gets to replace Fern is as much fun, he thought as he downed his drink in one gulp, ignoring the tiny voice inside that said he should feel some small remorse for the woman who lay so close to death. As Sprigs looked around the room, he noted a card game going at a table with a couple of guys that he knew. He headed that way to join the game. The rest of the day, that's where he stayed. The women in the room tried to look like they weren't avoiding him and the men luckily seemed to be doing their damndest not to anger him.

Later that evening, Doc Adams walked into the saloon looking for Hank.

"Sorry to have to tell you this, Hank, but Fern didn't make it. Her injuries were just too severe."

Hank looked at the floor as he tried to keep anger at bay. Fern brought in money for him but he had liked her too.

"Thanks for all you did for her, Doc. I know you at least made her comfortable in the end. I uh…hell, I suppose I need to go let the other girls know." He shook the doc's hand, unexpected, tears brimming in his eyes.

After the doctor left, Hank stood up on the bar and waited for everyone to notice him. "Everyone quiet down. Fern just died," he announced.

The party atmosphere of moments before, became sober.

Sprigs' voice boomed throughout the room. "Well shit, doesn't mean the party's gotta stop. Ken, a round of drinks for the house."

Ken started filling shot glasses but stopped . The men were slowly, quietly gathering up their belongings and walking out the swinging doors.

"Hey, come on, where the hell is everyone goin'," Sprigs shouted.

"Sprigs, shut the hell up, you bastard. Ain't you got no respect?" one of the departing men grumbled.

The women all huddled together crying, arms around one another. The ones who were still allowing Fern's death to sink in, passed on the news to the men and women that were coming down the stairs. That evening the saloon closed early as the men went home to their families or bunkhouses and the women commiserated with one another, sharing memories of Fern.

Chapter Eleven

Rayne rode into the yard in front of her place and immediately felt that something was off. She dismounted slowly and tethered her horses to the fence. She pulled her gun out of its holster, and walked into the barn where she lit a lantern. Her eyes gazed at her surroundings and she saw nothing out of place. With lantern in hand, she headed toward the small house.

Stepping onto the front porch, she immediately saw a window broken out. Lucifer sniffed the ground and walked into the house ahead of Rayne. She entered with the gun held high and stood behind Lucifer. She watched him as he trotted through the house looking for any uninvited guests. When he returned and sat by her feet, she lowered her gun and finally took a good look around. What she saw made her blood run cold. Lamps and tables were overturned and the chairs had ragged cuts in them. The dishes in the kitchen were scattered and broken on the floor. The windows in her bedroom were broken with the bed torn apart, and the blankets cut to shreds.

Rayne, not bothering to look at any more, turned on her heel and headed back toward the front yard. She un-tethered the horses and led Apache and Delilah into their stalls. Rayne jumped into Samson's saddle, hollered at Lucifer to stay, and kicked the horse into a

gallop, leaving a cloud of dust behind her as rode toward town.

†

As soon as she arrived in town, Rayne immediately went to Sheriff Kennedy's office and found a deputy she didn't know minding the office.

"Can I help you, ma'am?"

"Where's Sheriff Kennedy? I need to speak with
him immediately."

"Ma'am you need to calm down so that I can understand you." The officer stood.

"Calm down hell, you need to get the sheriff, right
now."

"Ma'am...you're the Mathews woman ain't ya?"

Rayne nodded.

"Look, I'm Sam, Kennedy's deputy. Now you can
tell me what happened and we'll go from there, okay?"

"Someone wrecked my house, went in, and tore
the hell out of it. That's what happened."

"Let me get my horse and I'll meet you outside
and we will go get the sheriff."

The sheriff opened his door and looked at his
deputy and Rayne. "Come on in. What's goin' on?"

"Someone broke into my house while I was gone
and tore it apart."

"When did you leave?"

"Yesterday mornin'."

Tom scratched his nose. "Well the way I see it,

Rayne, it bein' so dark and all there is not much we can do tonight. Why don't you get you a room at Bessie's place and tell her it is on me. Then tomorrow we can all ride out to your place and get a good look at what happened."

"Guess I have no choice." Rayne sighed in resignation.

Rayne went to Bessie's for a meal and a room for the night. After arranging for the room, Rayne walked into the dining room, found a table, and sat down.

A young, red haired girl approached her. "What can I get cha?" she asked.

"Steak, potatoes, and coffee."

Before long, Bessie walked over and took a seat across from her.

"Hey, how are you? How's that place of yours comin' along?"

"Oh, hi, Bessie. The place…well, it was looking good."

Bessie took a good long look at Rayne. "Girl, you look wrung out, what do you mean it *was* lookin' good?"

"Someone broke into my house and threw everything around."

"Oh, honey, that is terrible."

"Yeah. A good thing happened though. I went over to Cherokee Falls to buy some cows and ran into a man and his wife who were good friends of my aunt and uncle. The man said he came from Boston with Uncle Luke when they were young."

"That's nice that you met some friends of your

aunt and uncle. Treasure them, Rayne. I'll bet they got the memories they'd love to share. As for your house, I'm sure sorry to hear about that, Rayne. You best be careful till you find out who done it."

"So what's been going on? It's been a while since I was in town," Rayne asked trying to get her mind off her troubles.

"Well, poor Fern died.

"Who was Fern?"

"She was a working girl over at the saloon. Story is, Hank went looking for her and found her in her room close to death's door."

Bessie leaned closer to Rayne. "She'd been badly beaten. Lots of people are sayin' the last person she was seen with was that Jeremiah Sprigs. He denies it, of course. And Sheriff Kennedy hasn't done anything but question the man."

"Well surely the Sheriff would do something if he had proof. He seems to be a right fair man to me."

"Oh, I ain't speakin' ill of the sheriff at all. Don't think I am, please. It seems to me it fits, and poor Fern ain't in no position at all to say who done her in."

"When did all this happen?" Rayne asked.

"Oh, last night. Little old Fern passed on late this afternoon. Hank closed the saloon for the night. The other girls are takin' her passing right hard."

"That's too bad," Rayne said, frowning. "I sure am sorry for their loss. Losin' someone ain't an easy thing," she added quietly. She was thinking about her Aunt Martha and Uncle Luke and the other people who she hadn't lost to death—the ones that were no longer in her life due to choices she had had to make. Yes, losing someone didn't always have to mean losing them to death.

"Well, here comes your dinner. You eat and relax, all right? I'm sure the Sheriff and Deputy Sam will get to the bottom of your troubles in the morning. I assume you already got yourself fixed up with a room for the night?"

"I sure did. Can't say I wasn't lookin' forward to my own bed, but if I gotta stay somewhere else then I can't think of a place with a softer bed." Rayne gave Bessie a small smile.

"Good, now you go on and eat your dinner and we'll talk later. Seems I'm being called." Bessie nodded to the table of women over in the corner. She leaned in and whispered, "Most likely they want gossip. I swear some of these women ain't got nothin' better to talk about."

Rayne watched as Bessie approached the table with a big smile. She shook her head knowing deep inside that Bessie loved knowing the latest gossip just as much as the others did.

Later, after she had finished her dinner, Rayne decided to head over to the livery and make sure Samson had his dinner and was set for the night. She knew Lucifer and her other horses had plenty of food and hay to make it through the night. The walk in the warm night air felt good and relaxing. She could smell the clean fresh night air that held a hint of summer. Since the nights were still cool, there was crispness in the night air and some far off homesteads had smoke drifting from chimneys.

The stars were bright and clear in the sky; the moon, almost full, was a sight to see.

God, I love being out in the open where I can see the beauty of all of this, she thought as she walked.

As she strode across the street, she spied a short young woman with moonlight shining off her blonde hair. It made Rayne's heart stop beating. Could this be the woman from her dreams? *Oh, get it together, Rayne. She is imaginary,* a part of her murmured, but a bigger part of her said she was real and waiting for her to find her. Rayne rushed across the street to catch up with the young woman but missed seeing which building she entered.

"Damn, where'd she go? She couldn't have gone into the saloon since it's closed." She reasoned as she looked up and down the street. The mercantile and all the other buildings along the street were closed as well. The only place with shining lights was Bessie's and she had just come from there. "Damn."

Chapter Twelve

Emma had ducked out of the saloon that evening even before it closed. She needed to think and she wanted to mourn Fern alone. Fern had been someone that truly cared about her and had taken care of her after her mother died. She had been the one who held her each night as she cried, missing her mama. The others helped out, but Fern was the only one she allowed to get close to her heart.

As she sat on the little knoll outside the church gazing at the moon, she prayed that someone would come and take her away from the life that was waiting for her. She knew what fate had in store for her and she feared she would end up as Fern had—alone and dying in a puddle of her own blood. She didn't care who rescued her but hoped it would be the raven-haired blue-eyed woman, whose strong arms held her and comforted her in her dreams.

"Stop it, Emma. She isn't real and even if she was, do you think she would ever want to take care of you and love you once she finds out where you come from?" she said aloud as she walked back toward the saloon. Oblivious to the beauty of the night, she went in, closed the door, and walked up the narrow stairs to her room where she cried for Fern and for not having the woman of her dreams.

The next few days were a flurry of activity for Emma as she dealt with the day-to-day activities that life threw at her. She was learning how to work the floor of the saloon and was constantly under either the watchful eye of Hank or that of Sprigs. Emma was afraid of the man everyone thought murdered Fern and did everything she could to avoid him. However, when Hank told her to stop avoiding his best customer, Emma knew that Sprigs had said something to her boss.

A few days later, Emma realized her worst fears as she walked into the saloon and saw Hank and Jeremiah Sprigs speaking in hushed tones. She saw them look at her and the grin on Jeremiah's face made her shiver. She knew from Fern that he liked to be rough and to hurt women. Even though no one could be positive that Fern hadn't been up in her room with someone after Sprigs, Emma knew in her heart that Sprigs was the man responsible for her friend's death. She had tried all week long to avoid the man and not bring his attention to her, a task harder than she thought it would be. Now, it appeared as if her time of reprieve had run out.

Hank was walking toward her, and she couldn't quite define the look on his face. As he walked toward her, Sprigs' smile grew bigger which scared her even more.

"Em, it's time. I need you to go upstairs and entertain this man. Do whatever he wants, ya hear?"

"But, Hank, him? I don't think...."

"Go on and don't sass me, girl. He's paying big for you. "

With no choice, Emma walked toward Sprigs while Hank stormed to his office.

†

Hank tried all he could think of to get Sprigs to choose someone else. He knew how important his money was to keeping the bar healthy but he also knew what the man was capable of and he knew the damage he could cause. That was an experience he didn't want for Emma but Sprigs had his mind made up on this and there was no changing it.

"Well, shit!" he growled as he threw his half empty glass of whiskey at the wall.

Emma plastered a fake smile on her face. "Good evening, Mr. Sprigs." She couldn't stop her voice from shaking as underlying fear coursed through her.

"Evening, Miss Emma, it's downright nice of you to agree to share your company with me tonight." Sprigs' voice oozed with charm.

"Yes, well…how could I refuse such a kind offer." *Like there was no way I could get out of it,* she thought to herself.

"Well, shall we head upstairs?" Sprigs asked.

"Wouldn't you like another drink first? I would be happy to get you something."

"Now that sounds good. In fact, why don't we just get a bottle to take up with us?"

"Of course, as you wish."

Emma knew her time had just run out. She headed toward the bar with Sprigs behind her. A part of her had hoped she would be able to run and get away tonight, but she knew that would only delay the inevitable and make Hank angry with her. She resigned herself to her fate and smiled weakly as the young man behind the bar handed her a bottle of whiskey. Then Emma turned toward the staircase and the nightmare of her new life.

Chapter Thirteen

For several days, Rayne was busy replacing windows and repairing what items in her house that she could. When she first had come back from town, she and Tom had ridden around her ranch looking for suspicious tracks. They found none. Then the cows arrived and she spent time settling the herd into their new pastures. The days were long and at night she had the feeling of a good hard day's work behind her and she knew she had earned those tired, restful nights.

Each day started with her riding the fence to make sure no breaks had occurred. Throughout the week, Rayne had tended to the plowing and planting and decided it was time to head back into town. She needed more supplies, including a couple more planks of lumber to finish repairing a broken stall and enough extra for a rough dining table.

Rayne decided she was tired of her own cooking and figured she could spare enough for a drink at the saloon along with a nice dinner and one night at Bessie's place. Just the thought of the steak and potatoes Bessie served was making her mouth water. Truth was, she missed talking to Bessie. Rayne smiled as she realized that she considered Bessie her friend—she couldn't say she had a lot of those.

While sitting on Apache and surveying her land,

Rayne made the decision that she would head out early and stop off and see Mark and Emily. She wanted to thank them again for taking care of Apache and Delilah when she had gone to Cherokee Falls for her cattle. Once decided, she lightly kicked Apache in the flanks and tugged on the reins and the horse trotted toward the house.

Rayne grabbed her towel and a bar of soap, clean pants, and shirt, and headed toward the creek that ran behind her house. Given the heat of the day, she couldn't wait to feel the cold water on her skin. Sure enough, once she stripped her clothes off and walked into the deeper part of the creek, she felt the cold water flowing like ice over her and cooling her down completely.

"Yup, this is gonna be quick," she told herself, teeth chattering.

She quickly lathered the soap, washed her hair, and her body before rinsing the soap off and running out of the stream to dry off. Lucifer, who was lying on the ground, kept watch over her.

✝

It was mid-day when Rayne made it into town. Her first stop was at Gillum's where she placed her order. It wasn't long before she, the storeowner and the sheriff were deep in conversation.

"How's the house looking there, Rayne? Sure was sorry to hear about the going on's out there," Cyrus said.

"Starting to look like home again, and thank you for your concern. Tell ya what I sure do wish to hell I knew…who had it in for me bad enough that they'd destroy my house."

"Howdy, Sheriff, how are ya?" Cyrus said as the tall man walked up to the counter.

"Howdy, Cyrus, doin good. How about yourself? How are you, Rayne?"

"Doing fair," Rayne shook hands with the sheriff. "Any leads on who paid me a visit the other night?"

Tom shook his head and placed his order on the counter." I have some ideas but I ain't ready to talk about them yet," he replied, his attitude letting Rayne know the subject was closed.

"I'll be back later for my order, Cyrus," Tom said as he moved toward the door.

"I'll get mine tomorrow morning…I'm spending the night in town for a change. See you both later," Rayne said turning toward Mark's office

†

Mark looked up and immediately smiled. He liked Rayne and was glad she had stopped by. They spoke for a bit and Mark gladly closed his office for an hour so that he could accompany Rayne to his home. In all honesty, he was happy for the interruption and he was always willing to head home to see his pretty wife. Rayne had just given him a reason to do so.

The three enjoyed their visit and before long, evening was falling and Rayne decided it was time to say goodbye even though they repeatedly asked her to join them for dinner and offered her the use of the guest room.

"No. Thank you for the invitations but I thought I'd stop in and see an old friend."

"Rayne, I don't like you being out anywhere all alone especially since the other night," Emily said.

"Rayne, I have to agree," Mark added. "But I understand you wanting to have a normal life. Just be careful, please."

"Rayne, please reconsider." Emily watched as Rayne stood and placed her hat on her head.

"It's a very kind offer, and I promise I'll take you up on one of your fine dinners. For now, I best be heading on out." Rayne stepped off the porch where they had been sitting enjoying the late afternoon warmth.

✝

Rayne decided her next stop was going to be the saloon. She hadn't had a hard drink in quite a while and it was time the people got used to seeing her stop in from time to time. The piano was playing loudly in the corner and the combination of laughter and talking filled the room. Scattered tables with men playing cards peppered the room as well as women dressed in frilly, tight fitting dresses. The women were either serving drinks, sitting on laps, flirting, or had their hands on a particular man's shoulder.

With her hair up in her hat allowing no one to see her long tresses, Rayne was certain that everyone would ignore her, figuring she was a man. She walked up to the bar and ordered a whiskey before turning to look around. Soon she spotted a vacant table and, picking up her drink, she decided to sit there. Rayne's view from the table let her see most of the saloon and she enjoyed watching everything that was going on. She spotted a couple of card sharks and quickly learned which players to stay away from and which ones were actually in it for the draw of the game.

She had been studying a particular man and his game when all of a sudden, the hair on the back of her neck stood up and her eyes traced to the staircase. A beautiful blonde woman was coming down the stairs, her complexion and eyes marred by tears that streamed down her cheeks shimmering over the telltale redness of embarrassment. Behind her walked Sprigs, with a huge smirk of total satisfaction.

Sprigs walked toward a table where a couple of his grimy workers sat and announced. "I've just taught that woman a thing or two about how a man likes things. She's a good little piece."

The comment made the woman turn even redder. She looked away.

Hank turned and looked at Sprigs. "Leave her alone, Sprigs. Why don't you just go home?"

Sprigs glared at Hank.

Something in Rayne snapped. She silently stood,

walked over to where Sprigs sat with his smug looking face and one hand wrapped possessively around the girl's arm.

"Yep, I gotta say I think I broke her in real good. Though, I might have to have another go at her after a while and see if she learned anything."

Rayne wrapped her fingers around Sprigs' shirt, yanked him up, and spun him around forcing him to let go of the girl.

The surprised look on Sprigs' face quickly turned to anger.

Before he could react, Rayne punched him square in the face and Sprigs fell to the floor in a heap. The two men with him stood so fast that their chairs tumbled to the floor. Both reached for their guns.

Rayne's cold, clear blue eyes dared them to pull out their guns. "Go ahead. Let's see how fast you are," Rayne growled.

Both men shook their heads and grabbed for Sprigs. They pulled him up and carried him out of the bar.

Rayne took off her hat and wiped the sweat from her brow. When her long black hair fell around her shoulders, she remembered where she was. She looked around and saw everyone in the saloon looking at her and murmuring quietly to one another. Rayne walked toward the blonde, grabbed her hand, and led her out of the saloon.

✝

When Hank heard Sprigs snide comments and saw Emma's tear streaked face, he wasn't so sure he had made the best decision in letting Sprigs take her upstairs. He felt like shit over it. His greatest desire at that moment was for Sprigs to leave and never come back.

Deep inside, Hank held great appreciation for what the woman had done. She had come to Emma's rescue and put Sprigs in his place and Hank felt ashamed that he hadn't the courage to do the same. He decided that Rayne would always be considered a friend and be treated as such. He never really wanted Emma to be one of the girls or end up like Fern. He should have known that with Sprigs interested in her, Emma didn't stand a chance.

Chapter Fourteen

Rayne, not yet saying a word, walked with the blonde back toward her room at Bessie's place. They entered the boarding house, walked up the stairs, and into her room where she sat the woman down and draped a blanket around her shoulders. Despite the warmness of the night, the young woman was shaking.

"You don't need to be afraid now," she told the girl. "It's going to be okay. I won't let that man or any man do that to you again. I'm going to arrange for some food and a bath for you. Is that okay?" Rayne spoke in a calm, tender voice with her eyes never leaving the girl's face.

Emma nodded.

"I won't be long." Rayne desperately wanted to pull the girl into a hug but knew it was not the time. She left the room and headed down the stairs to find Bessie.

"Bessie will you bring a warm meal up to my room and prepare a hot bath?"

"Sure will. You ain't eatin' in the dining room?"

"No. Look, I was over at the saloon and I saw this working girl being totally humiliated by Sprigs and it made me so mad, I punched him and pulled her out of the place. She's up in my room now and I would appreciate it if you could go to the room with me and sit with her until I get back."

"Not a problem. Let me order the meal and arrange the bath and I will be right with you."

Rayne tapped lightly on the door before she opened it. "How are you doin'? This here is my friend, Bessie, and she is going to stay with you while I take care of something. She's real nice so you don't have to be afraid. Is that okay with you?"

The girl nodded and Bessie made her way toward her. "You poor child. I've got some soup and bread comin' for you and the bath is getting ready."

Once she saw that the girl was accepting Bessie's presence, Rayne left the room.

Rayne walked back to the saloon needing to speak to Hank. She found the man behind the bar.

"Can we speak in private?" She saw surprise on his face.

"Sure, let's go to my office."

"I wanna apologize for my actions earlier. I'm not ashamed that I hit him, but that I did it in here. I should have taken it outside. I don't know what the woman's name is but I can promise you, sure as I'm standin' here, that she will not be returning. So, if you feel I owe you anything, speak now and I'll compensate you for a night or two. Otherwise, I'll expect to not hear how I cheated you or anything like that on the streets."

"Now, Miss, I can assure you ya ain't gonna hear nothin' bad from me. I want ya to know that putting Emma out on the floor to work was honestly the last thing I wanted to do, especially once I knew old Sprigs had an eye out on her."

"Her name is Emma?"

Hank nodded. "Any money I took from them girls went to feedin' and clothin' em, nothin' more. With Fern gone and Emma not bringin' nothin' in…well, I just couldn't see a way to make it all work. I'm still short a girl but it's better that it's not her. With her now in your care…" he eyed Rayne. "She is in your care now, right?"

"Yeah, I suppose she is. I'll see to her needs from now on," Rayne answered.

"Right then, with you takin' care of her I ain't gotta worry about it, and well, I thank ya for gettin' her out of Sprigs' way. Can't prove it, but I know it was him that did Fern in." He looked down at the floor.

"Well, if he did…trust me he'll pay. No way will he do the same to Emma."

"Thank you." Hank put his hand out.

Rayne took his hand and shook it. "No need to thank me. Something about Sprigs just made me see red when I heard what he said coming down those stairs and I saw the look on her face. Ain't no need to talk that way 'bout anyone." Rayne shook her head and turned to leave.

"Miss Mathews, anytime you're in town, please stop by. Your next beer is on the house."

"That's mighty nice of ya. I'll do that."

Rayne, for the first time, took a good look at Hank's face trying to see if the man meant what he'd just said. With a good feeling, she realized he did.

Chapter Fifteen

Rayne walked back into the boarding house and found Bessie waiting for her and motioning her to join her. Rayne walked into the dining room and sat down with Bessie.

"How is she?"

"As good as can be expected, poor child. Look, I know you're new in town and wouldn't know this but that poor girl has been through a lot,"

"Okay, so tell me about it."

"Well, her name is Emma Rodgers. She lost her ma when she was only a year old. Seems her folks were passing through and her pa died on the trail and her ma ended up here sick and dyin' too, probably childbed fever. One of the girls that worked for Hank found 'em both. Wasn't long after that her ma passed and Fern took a likin' to the child and raised her. Now, don't you go holding Hank to blame for nothin'. He was only doin' what he had to…."

"Bessie, I already spoke to Hank."

"All right then. So what are ya gonna do now, young lady?"

"When I pulled her out of there, I guess I sort of assumed responsibility for her. So I take her home and provide for her if that's what she wants."

"Em and I spoke a bit. Now mind you, she is

scared and upset and well, it bein' her first time and all…well, any ways, she is of the mind that she is sticking with you for the time bein'. She asked me if that was what you had a mind to do. Now, I told her I had no idea, but that you are a good woman. Rayne, make sure you realize exactly what it is you're doin' before you cause that child any more hurt, please."

Rayne nodded as she stood to leave. "I will never hurt her," she declared.

As she walked to her room, she did indeed think about what she was doing. She knew in her heart that there was no way in hell she could let that poor girl go back to the saloon and she knew she couldn't allow her to wander the streets. Something about the girl was calling to her and drawing her heart. *Emma is her name.* She had never met the woman before but her soul told her that she had known of her whole life.

As she approached the door, she stopped as the full ramification of what she had just accepted hit her. Taking a deep breath, she slowly opened the door and entered, feeling as though from this moment on her life would never be the same.

As Rayne opened the door to her room, she saw the girl, wrapped in a blanket, sitting on the bed. She looked up as Rayne walked in, and the moment their eyes met, Rayne felt as if their souls recognized one another. Every molecule in her body felt charged with electricity with the overwhelming need to protect the blonde.

"Thank you," Emma stated softly.

"For what? I didn't do anything."

"You did, you just don't know it yet."

"Well, um…I guess we need to decide where to go from here. I kinda feel like…well…"

"I don't have any place to go. I have no family and no money. I know you don't know me and you have no responsibility toward me, but I can't go back there. I'd be downright appreciative if I could go with you…at least until I figure out what to do." Emma's face turned pink.

"You're welcome to stay with me for as long as you want. As for goin' back to that place…I don't think so. That line of work ain't for you, and I'd die 'fore you went back there."

"So, um…think I can know your name?" Emma asked. She pulled the blanket around her tighter, before settling back on the bed, her eyes darting around the room.

"Oh, I'm sorry. I'm Rayne."

"Mathews? Luke and Martha… were they your kin?"

"Yeah…did you know 'em?"

"Enough to know they were good people. She always spoke to me never treated me differently than she did any other woman she encountered. Even though I was just a cleaning girl. Not like a lot of the other women around here."

"Yeah, that's what I'm hearing. Guess I missed out on getting to know 'em better. Shoot, last time I seen 'em I was only a sprout … maybe eight years old."

"So you're all right with me stayin' until I figure

out what to do?"

"Of course you're welcome to stay as long as you like. Mind you, it ain't much to look at right now but its home. I had to do some quick repairs the other day since it seems that someone decided it was a good idea to throw stones through my windows. I hope that don't scare ya off."

"Trust me, after the week I've had, I don't think broken windows will worry me much. Unless, of course, it's in the middle of the night. Then I'm sure you'll come runnin' cuz I promise I'll be screamin'." Emma shivered and pulled the blanket closer.

Rayne saw the terror cross Emma's face and kept her distance. "You're safe with me. Trust me, if anyone comes around in the middle of the night, ol' Lucifer will have them screamin'," Rayne said, smiling.

"Lucifer? Um, what or who is Lucifer?"

"Lucifer is my dog…well actually, he ain't mine. He just showed up one day and decided to stick around. Follows me like my shadow

"So you're kind of a beacon for strays?"

"Yeah, I suppose so." Rayne chuckled at that statement. "So, um, it's late and we need an early start in the mornin'. I suppose we should get some shut eye."

"Oh, of course. I'm sorry. I'm usually not so chatty. I just feel like I've known you all my life. I'll just settle down on the floor so you can have your bed." She started to rise.

"No, that's all right. You stay where you are. I'll sleep on the floor."

"No, I can't do that to you after all you done. Besides, I'm kinda still a little…I don't know…would you mind sharing the bed? I'd feel safe with you here and I think I might be able to sleep better if you were next to me." Emma stared at the blanket.

"Oh, well yeah, I'm sure you are …um…sure I can do that." Rayne's fingers immediately went to her hair, running through it as she looked nervously out the window unsure as to what to do.

Emma moved over and slid off the bed then pulled the blankets down before quickly sliding under them.

Rayne had seen how apprehensive Emma was and had turned to give the blonde some privacy. She moved to sit on the bed and slide her boots off, then slowly undid her shirt and pulled it off, stood to do the same to her pants, and then slid under the blankets still dressed in her long johns. She lay on her back staring at the ceiling. It felt so right being next to the other woman yet she was also uncomfortable. She rolled on to her right side and realized that was a mistake because now she faced Emma.

Just breathe, Rayne. It's all right. Sounds like she drifted off to sleep already anyway, so just relax.

Rayne eventually did slip off to sleep as well. That was only after she had thought of all the responsibility she had taken on when she said *yes* to Emma staying with her. She was now responsible for feeding, clothing, and providing shelter for another woman as well as protecting her. She realized suddenly that she didn't have a problem with any of it. In fact, she realized that she was actually looking forward to doing all those things. *What is it with this woman?* Rayne felt as if she found the other half of herself and that confounded her. She would look into Emma's eyes and see her own past in them. It was as if they had shared a life before. Her heart felt like it wanted to explode for some reason every time she looked at Emma.

Sometime during her night, Rayne rolled over and wrapped her arm around Emma.

Emma jumped and covered her body protectively. "Get your hands off me," she screamed.

Rayne sat straight up in the bed, her hand on the ivory handle of her 45.

"What…who's there?" she called.

Emma reached out with shaking fingers and touched Rayne. "I'm sorry. It was just a dream. Please put the gun down."

"You sure you're all right? It was just a dream?"

"Yes, I think you placed your arm around me and well…I was already dreaming and I'm sorry.…"

"Oh, God, I'm sorry. I didn't mean to…I.…"

"Rayne, it's all right. I'm sure you didn't mean anything by it, I overreacted because of what happened earlier tonight,"

"Did he hurt you?"

"Define hurt. He wasn't gentle by any means. God, I feel so ashamed,"

"Did he raise his hand to you as well? I've heard stories.…"

"Not this time. No. He said he was going easy, it being my first time and all…" Emma shivered. "He said that I was getting special treatment this time; that he needed to break me in easy." Emma wrapped her arms around her body. "Then he said he expected I'd eventually fill Fern's shoes mighty nicely."

"It was your first time?"

"Yes."

"That miserable bastard. I should have killed him."

"Rayne, if it hadn't have been him it would have been someone else. Hank made sure I understood that."

Rayne gently place her hand on Emma's shoulder only to have the woman jump back.

"What's wrong?"

"I just…sorry that hurt a bit."

"Can I see?" Rayne asked. At Emma's nod, Rayne gently moved the gown off Emma's shoulder. Rayne sucked in a deep breath when she saw the angry red outline of teeth. The injury was deep enough to have drawn blood in a few areas. The anger in Rayne boiled.

"Bastard," she swore under her breath. "Did Bessie see this?"

"No. She left me alone while I…cleaned up. I asked her to. But she was right outside the door. She said she wouldn't leave me any farther than that because she promised you she wouldn't leave me alone."

"Yes. She did promise. Before we leave, we need to have Doc Adams look at this. I wanna make sure it ain't infected."

"Okay."

"Look, we'd better get some shut eye. We'll need some extra time in the morning. Are you okay now? "

"Is it okay if I snuggle against you?"

"Yes." Rayne pulled Emma close.

✝

The next morning Rayne was up and getting coffee in the dining room when Sprigs walked in. Both his eyes had dark rings under them and there was no doubt that she had broken his nose.

Sprigs began to advance on her. "I'm gonna take care of you, bitch."

Two of the men with him grabbed him and held him back

"What the hell do you think you're doin'? Let me go, damn it. That bitch needs to be taught a lesson."

The room fell quiet.

Rayne looked around the room. She rose from the table where she was sitting and looked directly at Sprigs. "Nice look for ya there, Sprigs."

"You bitch. God, I can't wait to teach you a thing or two. You ain't no man and you ain't got the right to speak to me that way, and you sure as hell don't deserve no goddamned ranch. Why don't you sell me that place and let a real man show you how it's done? Better yet, marry me and I'll show ya how a man does a lot of things."

"If you're gonna teach me a thing or two like ya did last night…well damn, I suppose I should be downright scared. And if I thought you were any sort of man, I just might consider selling you my place, but I don't. So get this straight…in fact, all you men here that think my place is up for grabs, ya'll might wanna hear this too… my place *ain't for sale*."

Rayne fixed Sprigs with a cold hard look, her eyes filled with hatred "Now, Sprigs, if you still think ya can take me, let's go on outside. I don't wanna mess Miss Bessie's place up. Course, I just might be more of a man than you are, and it might be *you* that's afraid. If that's the case, why not go back outside and crawl under that rock you slithered out from."

†

Jeremiah turned a deep red and his two friends backed away from him. He turned on his heel and glared at them. "What the hell is wrong with ya? Get outta my way." With that, he stormed out of the dining room, a roar of laughter following him.

"What are you two lookin' at?" Sprigs spat at the two men once they were outside.

"Nothin', boss, just.…"

"Just what? That you two cowards didn't think to back me up in there?"

"Jeremiah, you obviously ain't seen that look in her eyes. I damn near guarantee you she'd just as well shoot ya than talk to ya, and we kinda like livin' right now."

"Shit, you two just turned chicken shit, so don't

go givin' me no damn excuses,"

"Yeah, well you walked out just as quick as we did," Norman Bigalow said.

Sprigs gathered Norman's shirt in one hand and pushed the man against the building then leaned in so they were face to face. Through gritted teeth he said, "Remember who I am, boy. I'll kick your ass from here to next Sunday. Everything I do, I do for a reason, I choose when and where that cunt learns not to fuck with me. Ya hear?"

The frightened man nodded.

"Good. Now, go get my horse."

Jeremiah was eager to buy the land that now belonged to that bitch. Who did she think she was trying to run a ranch anyway? It was a man's job. He made no secret of his intentions… that he wanted to be the owner of that ranch. Even when Luke Mathews was still alive, he made certain that everyone knew he wouldn't take kindly to anyone who tried to out bid him.

His eyes had spotted the tall woman when he walked into the room. Despite his broken nose, he had let his eyes roam up and down her body. What she had done to him the night before humiliated him but nevertheless, he felt a strong sexual stirring when he looked at the woman. *A man needs boys to carry on his name and I can kill two birds with one stone here.* His lips curled into a smile.

He touched his nose and grimaced.

"But first she will pay for embarrassing me," he said aloud.

Chapter Sixteen

As Rayne and Emma rode up to Rayne's place, Emma took in the beauty of it all. She could smell the sweet aroma of the prairie grass; she was able to hear the water of the flowing creek and the occasional moo of a cow. She spotted a dog trotting toward them as they stopped in front of the small, wood-frame house.

"Em…hey, do you mind if I call you Em?" Rayne asked as she helped Emma off the horse.

"No, not at all." Emma smiled. She liked the way it sounded coming from Rayne.

"Okay," Rayne said with her own big smile. "This here is Lucifer. Lucifer, this is Emma and she is gonna be stayin' with us for a spell."

Emma looked at the big dog that seemed to be studying her as he sniffed her hands. Emma reached out and patted the dog's head for just a minute before she watched him trot back to his spot on the front stoop.

"He's a funny dog that's for sure," Rayne said. She laughed before leading the horse toward the barn.

Emma followed Rayne and stood beside her when she stopped at a stall in the barn. She opened the stall and led Apache toward the corral to let him stretch his legs. She put Samson into his stall then took Delilah out to join Apache.

"This here is Apache and the lighter bay is Delilah. Apache here is my best friend. We rode out here together from back East." Rayne tenderly stroked the horse's mane then hugged him. "I love him, ya know? And it kills me that I know his time is getting' short."

"Well, hello there, Apache. My, aren't you a beautiful animal?" Emma got a snort from Apache for her comment.

Delilah's front hoof pawed at the ground.

"Oh, my yes, you are too, Delilah. I'm sorry to have neglected to mention that sooner, girl," Emma laughed. "It's like they understand what I'm saying."

"I should have warned you. Delilah is sort of touchy about things. She seems to feel the need to be the center of attention. Don'tcha girl?"

Rayne ruffled Delilah's ears and chuckled. "I got her at the same time I got Samson; she was glued to his side and wouldn't allow me near him without her bein' involved. It was so cute I just didn't have the heart to separate em."

"How did Apache deal with two new arrivals in his stable?"

"He don't mind none. I think he likes the idea that he ain't gotta go out and pull the plow or herd the cattle as much."

"Oh well. I can understand that." Emma moved so she was standing in front of Delilah, petting her ears. "I don't blame ya none at all, Apache."

"Come on, I'll show you the house then I need to come back out and feed the critters."

Emma walked behind Rayne as they exited the

barn. "Let me help with that. I might as well start earning my keep around here."

"No, that's all right. I got it…."

"Rayne, look, you did me a big favor by taking me out of that saloon, and I don't expect to stay with you and let you do all the work. Not when I'm able to help. I can cook and clean the house for you, make sure you got clean clothes, and I'll help you tend to the animals and whatever else needs tendin' to."

"I figured we'd get to that later. But if ya wanna help…sure come on. First thing we need to do is unsaddle Samson and brush him down. I'll do that if you wanna give ole Apache and Delilah a bucket of oats." Rayne spoke as she walked toward the barn with Emma following her.

The two began working side by side getting the few chores done in very little time. Rayne finished her part first, and then showed Emma the rest of the barn before heading for the house.

Inside the house, Rayne said, "Well this is it, this is home." Pride was in her voice but she knew it was mixed with a little nervousness.

"It's cozy, the feeling of home does come through in the way it's been set up," Emma commented.

"This here is the kitchen obviously, and that there leads to the store room," Rayne said as she pointed out a door.

"This door over here is the bedroom. Uh, I suppose we'll have to figure out who's sleepin' where." Rayne stated nervously as she walked toward the bedroom. "I know for a fact that the ground and floor ain't comfortable at all. So, um…if you don't mind…I guess we share the bed. That is until I can figure something else out."

"Well, that's just fine. I shared a bed at Hank's all the time. I don't mind if you don't."

"It's only till I figure out how to fix the problem,"

Emma nodded and walked back to the fireplace. "This is where you cook right?"

"Yes, my aunt preferred it to a stove."

"It'll take some getting used to."

Rayne looked around nervously wondering what to do next. "Well, that's about it." She looked away. "I need to head out to the canyon and see how the rest of my cattle are doin'."

"Wait, what…do you have to leave now? How long will you be gone?"

"Well, I leave now and I'll be back late tonight."

"Do you really have to go now? I mean I just got here and Sprigs will be lookin' for me." Emma wrapped her arms around her waist. "That scares me."

"I'm sorry. I wasn't thinking." Rayne looked down at her feet, her face red with embarrassment. "I can check on them in the morning and maybe you can go with me and ride Delilah."

"I don't know how to ride. Coming out here was the first time I was ever on a horse."

"Oh." Rayne looked at the frightened woman. "Then I'll leave at first light and be back as fast as I can."

†

The next morning as Rayne saddled Apache, she thought about Emma.

The afternoon and evening went by fast just doing chores around the place and she was amazed by the way Emma just stepped up and helped without a complaint. Most of the women she'd known hated to be around any animals. She grinned. They were mostly working women and they had made it clear they had no plans on taking care of any animals except maybe the men they served. Truth be told, she had never had occasion to ask any of them. She stole a glance at the house. *Hell, none of 'em ever made my heart skip a beat like Emma does. What is it about this one?* She didn't know the answer but only knew that every time she looked at or thought about Emma it made her soul dance.

"God, I need to figure this out, Apache." She flicked the reins and lightly kicked the horse's flanks. "Come on, let's take a ride."

The big bay took off at a gallop.

†

From the small kitchen window, Emma watched as Rayne and the bay rode off toward the south. She had a mixture of feelings going through her. Along with relief and thankfulness, she felt other things as well. While sitting behind Rayne on the horse as they rode to the house, she had a feeling that she had done it before. There was a security and a feeling of belonging in that simple action. Every time Rayne looked into her eyes, Emma was filled with a warmth she'd never felt before. She was sure she would never feel that way with anyone else since there was something about Rayne that called to her. She couldn't put a finger on it or explain what it was she felt, however.

She did know that Rayne made her feel as if a part of her long forgotten self was coming alive. To feel the woman's hands simply brush her, for the simplest of reasons, caused her body to feel things that it had never felt before.

"Oh, boy. I'd better figure this one out quick," she told herself.

She took one last look out the window before turning away. Her eyes gazed over the cabin's interior and she felt her shoulders relax. "Now, what shall I do next?"

Chapter Seventeen

From the rim of the canyon, a lone figure watched as Rayne rode through a narrow pass. With his rifle aimed and steady, his one thought was how easy it would be to kill the bitch. *One shot and all my problems would be over. The ranch would revert to the bank and I can take possession of it.* With the prime prairie grass and the creek that ran through it, he knew his cattle would fatten quickly.

"No, not yet," he murmured aloud.

He got up from his prone position and his body protested—he'd been lying there for well over an hour. He walked to his horse and stuck his rifle in the scabbard before leading the horse farther away from the rim to minimize the chance of the bitch seeing him when he climbed into the saddle. He couldn't afford for her to suspect he was watching her.

He figured that soon he'd be able to start rustling some of the cattle without leaving any traces of his being there. It wouldn't be long before the ground would freeze so hard that there would be no trail to follow. He knew of a shallow spot in the creek where he could herd the cattle across to a break in the fence.

"Very soon," he mumbled. He thought about how close he had been that one time when his plan to get hold of the land was going so well. Wilson, the sniveling coward at the bank, was about to foreclose on the land and had assured him once that happened the spread would be his. Then, from out of the blue, old Mathews up and paid off the balance a week before it was due. Wilson told him there was no way he could get his hands on the place after that.

Then, fate jumped in and Mathews and the old lady had died. He figured he could pick the ranch up for next to nothing since there was no one to claim the land. It wasn't long after that Wilson informed him the place had been taken out of his hands since Matthews left the land to a relative who was about to show up. Wilson told him that Benton had opened an account and placed the money from the cattle he sold into the account. The banker told him the new owner was on his way to take possession.

Who would have guessed that the new owner was a woman?

Sprigs thought he could sweet talk and charm the woman into selling her land to him. But, she wasn't falling for it or interested in what he had to say so he had to formulate a new plan. It would take longer but it would work. *One way or another I'll own that land,* he thought.

✝

Rayne felt the hairs on her neck prickle and she looked up at both sides of the canyon's rim. She saw nothing. She rubbed the back of her neck and cautiously continued riding deeper into the canyon. The trees were already starting to change color and she knew it wouldn't be long before winter hit. She looked down at the ground close to creek bed to see if there were any shoed horse tracks. Not finding any, she increased Apache's gait and rode toward the herd. Her cattle were contentedly eating the sweet grass, drinking the cold water from the stream, and some were lying in the sunny areas. She grinned knowing that she made a good decision when she bought the cows. With a tug on the reins, she guided Apache over to the creek and followed it for a while before crossing the water. She rode to the fence line and she guided the bay along it at a steady pace. After she rode it for a good while, she came upon a broken length and frowned.

"I'm sure I fixed this part of the fence," she murmured.

Rayne got off Apache and walked closer to the fence before crouching to inspect the wire. Sure enough, someone had pulled the wire off and then lightly tacked it back into place so it would appear structurally sound. It was unfortunate that the ground on that side of the creek was hard and dry, making any tracks invisible.

"Well, shit." Rayne set her jaw and strode with purpose toward her horse and her saddlebags. With her pliers and gloves in hand, she moved quickly to mend the fence. "This time I'm gonna have to fix it so it won't come undone again." Her eyes scanned the area hoping to glimpse the person responsible.

After counting the herd, Rayne was thankful none

were missing. *I'm still going to have to go to the sheriff about this,* she thought anxiously.

Assured that the mend to the fence was sufficient so that the cattle wouldn't get out, Rayne mounted Apache and headed toward home.

The thought of home and Emma being there made her smile and she nudged Apache on to an easy gallop.

Chapter Eighteen

The late afternoon sun hit her back causing the sweat to drip from her face and soak the collar of her shirt. She had just ridden up to the house and was walking toward the barrel of water, when she heard Lucifer growl. Rayne looked up and saw one of the men that had been with Sprigs the night before riding toward her. She instinctively lowered her hand to the 45 strapped to her waist.

"Relax, ma'am, I ain't got no beef with you," the man said as he got close. "'Sides I think that dog of yours would kill me fore you even cleared leather." The man got off his horse.

"What do you want, mister?" Rayne held her ground with her hand resting on the hilt of her gun.

"Name's Roger MacMillan. Like I said, I ain't got no quarrel with you…just wanted to make that clear. You need to know that Sprigs seems to have a burr under his saddle where you're concerned and I think ya need to watch your back."

"Why are you warnin' me?"

"Cuz he's got something in the works. He ain't telling any of us about it, being real close to the vest about it all. But, he don't like you none at all. That he's real clear about."

"I ain't got no love for him either,"

"Miss Mathews, I ain't sure you're gettin' my drift here. He'd soon as see you dead as he would look atcha."

"Yeah, well, not much I can do about that, now is there?"

"No, I suppose not, but I just wanna make sure you is clear on me not havin' no part of it."

"Look, Mr. MacMillan, I don't intend on endin' up dead just yet, and I do thank ya for lettin' me know. I'll keep in mind you tryin' to warn me an' all. Now, if there's nothin' else, I'd like to go in and grab some dinner before I have to tend to the rest of my ranch."

"Oh, yeah, sure. Sorry. I didn't mean to interrupt nothin'. Like I said, I just wanted to let ya know." The lanky man turned to mount his horse and began to ride away only to be stopped by Rayne's voice.

"Hey, MacMillan, you know anything about visitors to the canyon? Seems someone decided to loosen some wire that marks the boundary and keeps my herd in place."

"Nah, I ain't got any idea. But sounds to me like you're fixin' to have a whole heap of troubles on ya." The man spurred his horse and rode off.

"Well that's just dandy…" Rayne muttered as she entered the small house.

"Hope you're hungry," Emma said.

Rayne saw Emma looking up from the fireplace and smiled. The table was set with two places, and two cups of milk sat at each setting.

Emma was pulling ham steaks and mashed potatoes from kettles over the fire and she placed filled bowls on the table. She then went back for the biscuits, poured gravy into a bowl and set these items on the table as well.

"I sure am." Rayne's mouth was watering when she saw the bounty on her table. "Wow, you did all this with what I had in the house?"

"Well…yes, of course. And there is peach cobbler for dessert as well," Emma answered with a smile.

"Are you serious? Where did you find it all? I mean I…" Rayne was overwhelmed with what she saw. "Lord, it smells great in here.'

"Sit down, Rayne, and eat before it goes cold."

Rayne readily complied. With her first mouthful of food—the flavors exploding in her mouth—her eyes closed and she groaned softly. The potatoes tasted of creamy butter, salt, pepper, a hint of garlic, and onion. The ham was tender and seasoned perfectly as was the gravy. "Lord, Emma, these biscuits are so light and fluffy they almost melt in my mouth." She let out a satisfied sigh. "I've never tasted anything as delicious as this before.

Every so often Rayne looked at Emma, who had a distinct look of satisfaction on her face. Her eyes tracked to the window and saw that the sun slipping toward the western horizon. Its rays shining through the clouds, cast the sky in pink and violet colors with occasional yellow streaks of sunlight reaching the ground. Rayne reluctantly stood before Emma got up to get the dessert. "Sorry, Em, I need to do the rest of my chores before the cobbler."

"I'll help you." Emma also stood.

"I'd like that." Rayne smiled and opened the door for Emma to walk out first.

"We need to feed the horses and throw fresh straw down in their stalls, and settle them for the night. It shouldn't take long."

"Let's get started then. We have cobbler waiting for us when we're done."

Within an hour, they finished their chores and headed back to the house.

"Sit, Rayne, and I'll fetch the coffee and cobbler."

"I still can't believe you found all the ingredients in my kitchen."

"Did you know you have a root cellar?"

Rayne shook her head.

"Well you do and your aunt put up peaches, apples, rhubarb, and all sorts of vegetables. I'd say it is enough to last for at least a year."

Rayne looked at Emma. "I thought I knew every part of the house…where did you find a root cellar?"

"Well, I was in the pantry lookin' for something' to make for dinner. It occurred to me that your aunt probably put up some fruits and vegetables so I began looking around. I saw a stack of bushel baskets and when I moved them I saw a door and opened it. After I lit a lamp and went down the stairs I found all the jars."

Rayne shook her head and chuckled. "Amazing, you'll have to show me where it is. I can't believe I didn't see it all those summers I stayed here. Anyway, that was a delicious meal. Thank you."

"You're welcome. I take that, from the way you

ate, it's been a while since you had cobbler."

"God, yes. My mom use to make it…." Rayne tamped down her threatening emotions.

"What happened?" Emma whispered.

Rayne heard the softly spoken words and quickly shut down her emotions and shifted uncomfortably in her chair. She took a moment and cleared her throat.

"Thank you for the delicious meal. I was thinkin' I need to ride into town tomorrow to talk to the sheriff. Wanna go with me? If you don't want to, maybe I can stop by the saloon and pick up your clothes for you."

"Oh…I'm not sure…." Emma's eyes shifted to the floor.

"I know it's kinda soon for you to wanna go to town, but I figure the sooner you show you ain't afraid the better. I mean, I'll be with ya and all."

"I know that and I suppose you're right. Rayne, will you promise not to leave me alone?" Emma trembled.

Rayne locked eyes with Emma.

I've spent a lifetime searching for you. I will never again leave you alone.

Rayne felt conscious thought return and she reclaimed her mind. She suddenly felt very uncomfortable and looked away. *Where'd that come from?* Her eyes re-found Emma's face. "I'll stay beside you for as long as you need me to tomorrow."

"I'd like that."

"Good. If that's a plan then I suppose we should head on to bed."

"Of course. That sounds like a good idea." Emma

shifted her feet. "I need to do up the dishes first."

"I'll help you with the dishes."

Emma gathered the coffee cups and plates from their dinner and from the cobbler. After she set them down near the wash bucket she walked to the fireplace for the kettle she had placed on the hearth to heat before they sat down to eat. And with the glove that was near the hearth, she picked up the kettle and dumped it into a washbasin that contained cold water. She then began to wash their dinner dishes. She splashed the dishes all over with the water before using a rag to wash away the remnants of their meal.

Rayne grabbed a dry cloth and began drying the dishes as soon as Emma rinsed them. She stacked them on the shelf to the right of the window.

With the dishes done, there was nothing else to do but blow out the lantern they had burning on the table and head for the bedroom. Rayne turned down the lantern in the living area as well. Once in the bedroom, the two took off their clothes. Rayne, on one side, discarded her clothes and tossed them on the chair that sat in the corner before crawling under the covers. She covertly watched as Emma folded her clothes neatly before laying them at the foot of the bed. She felt the mattress shift as Emma lay down and pulled the covers over her.

"I had no idea how really tired I was," Emma mumbled. "Good night, Rayne."

"Good night, Emma." Rayne heard Emma's breath even out and knew she was asleep. Jumbled thoughts filled her mind as she too drifted off to a restless sleep…

Rayne felt the blonde clutching at her clothes with tears streaming down her face as she begged her not to go. It was Emma—she knew this without a doubt—but she was dressed in clothing from another time maybe even from another continent. It was hard to tell. Their home, lined with rock and sod, was more of a hut than anything else. There was a pit dug in the corner for warmth and cooking, and animal skins piled on the floor for bedding.

Rayne watched as the scene unfolded.

"Let the others go and fight. This isn't our battle, I beg of you to listen," the blonde cried.

"It is though, my love. If we don't fight for one another, who is there to fight for us? What they did to Marsh could happen to us just as easily. We were lucky it wasn't our home and livestock burned and killed,"

Rayne heard the words come out of her mouth yet she was unable to speak.

"And if you're killed, will Marsh see to your family…to your responsibilities here…will you have him see to me as well?"

"Will I be me if I don't go fight? You taught me the importance of standing up for one another and for honor. Does that all go away just because you fear I may die?"

"Honor means nothing if you're not alive to have it," the blonde spat out. She turned, opened the makeshift door, slamming it after she entered the hut.

"I'll be back; I swear I'll not leave you alone...."
Rayne watched as she climbed up on a steed and joined the group of men that were waiting on the knoll.

The mist was cold and dense, the fighting long and hard. Maybe her love had been right, she should have stayed out of it. The battle was one they couldn't...wouldn't win. She heard the screams of dying men, the hissing of arrows as they flew past her head. She never heard the man sneak up on her, all she remembered feeling was the blade of the knife plunging into her heart. In one unguarded, unsuspecting moment, all had been lost. With her dying breath, she remembered her words to the blonde, and knew it was a promise she would not be keeping...

Rayne woke with a start and a burning pain in her chest. The air she sucked into her lungs burned and sweat poured from her brow.

Emma bolted up in bed and immediately wrapped her arms around Rayne. "Shhh, it was just a dream. You're safe." She ran her hand down Rayne's long hair and soothed her with words.

She knew about the dreams—she'd had them too. It was always the same. Someone was always bringing a body back to her. She remembered waking from the dream in the same state as Rayne was in now. She recalled her heart breaking as she saw the dark-haired woman leave, and then breaking even more when a few straggling men returned with her body as well as so many other bodies.

The hate and bitterness she felt in those moments

fueled the hate and rage that kept her going through countless life times. Rayne calmed down in her arms and soon fell back to sleep. Emma slept fitfully until the light of dawn broke through the clouds and filled the room. With great care, she gently untangled herself from Rayne's tight embrace. After dressing quietly, she went through the bedroom door closing it softly behind her.

"It's a new day," she said softly as she smiled and made her way to the kitchen to make breakfast.

†

Rayne woke to the aroma of coffee and frying bacon, with vague remnants of the dream from the night before refusing to let go of her mind. She couldn't shake the feeling that it was more than just a dream. In her heart she knew that the blonde of her dream was Emma. As she dressed, she shook her head, trying to clear the cobwebs. Hard as she tried, she couldn't shake the memory that she had been *there* before. That thought alone left her shaken.

She walked out of the bedroom and saw Emma standing by the fireplace and again she was struck by a vision or memory so strong it nearly knocked her to her knees. A memory that took her back in time to when her dream took place....

Instead of the fireplace, Emma stood next to the crudely formed hearth with an infant in her arms. She

123

was quietly humming the baby to sleep.…

As quickly as the memory filled her mind, it was gone. Rayne was once again standing in her house with Emma standing in front of the fireplace humming. It was the same exact melody that she'd heard in the memory. Rayne took in a sharp breath.

Emma turned. She put the coffee pot down and rushed over to Rayne.

"What's wrong? Are you all right?" she asked. "You look pale. Come on, sit down."

She led Rayne to a chair. "Rayne, what's wrong? You're scaring me."

"I'm…I'm okay. I just I thought I saw something and it startled me a little more than I expected." Rayne let out a weak, shaky chuckle.

"Let me get you some coffee. It might help. Um, would you like some breakfast? I have bacon and some biscuits and I can fry up some eggs real quick."

"Just some coffee for the moment, thanks. Guess I'm still reelin' from a dream I had last night."

"Wanna talk about it? Sometimes it helps." Emma placed a cup of coffee in front of Rayne and sat down with her cup in her hand.

"I don't know…its strange…didn't feel like a dream really…not sure I can explain the feelin'. Felt kinda like I was there. Like it was real. Only it wasn't here or any place I've ever been. Hell, from what I could tell, I don't think it was even in this century. "

"What do you mean?"

"Felt like it was another lifetime and here's the

thing, you were in it. You were there beggin' me not to go."

"Go where, Rayne?"

"I don't know… don't remember the rest.…" Rayne didn't want to remember the rest. "Um how about we eat and then hitch the wagon to head to town. I need to talk to the sheriff and pick up a few things and some supplies I was supposed to get yesterday from Gillum's"

"Sure, of course. Would you like eggs?"

"Just some of those biscuits and bacon. It smells great and I'm hungry as a bear," Rayne said with a weak smile.

✝

Emma jumped up to grab the small breakfast and was pleased when Rayne ate well. She was afraid that Rayne would still be worried about the dream.

Once breakfast was finished, she watched as Rayne placed her hat on her head and went outside to hitch the wagon. Once done with her chores, Emma dried her hands on her skirt and looked around satisfied that the place was clean.

She walked toward the door with a smile knowing that with Rayne she would always be safe.

Chapter Nineteen

As they drove down the street, Emma felt the eyes of the town's folks on her and Rayne. She watched as many stopped and stared openly at them. She speculated that they all knew Rayne punched Sprigs and why she was now sitting next to Rayne. With their shoulders touching, Emma felt Rayne's back stiffen. It seemed to Emma that Rayne's hide had thickened tenfold and a wall immediately went up inside her making her sit straighter and taller. Yet, Emma felt a warmth and comfort emanating from Rayne as well. That gave her the strength to look the passersby straight in the eyes. A couple of ladies looked away as soon as Emma looked in their direction, but the majority looked straight at her and a few even smiled.

Emma knew she wasn't exactly an outcast in the eyes of the town's folks but close enough for them to scorn her. Everyone knew that her parents died and that Fern took her in and raised her in the bar and she knew many looked at her in that light. Even when she was only a child and didn't really understand why, she knew that some of the people in town treated her as nothing more than a saloon girl. As she got older, and understood what it meant to live at the saloon, she realized that many people thought that she would become or already was, just another girl who worked at the saloon, giving her body for money.

†

Rayne felt Emma's unease, as the wagon rolled down the middle of town. Her hand reached over and touched Emma's leg giving it a gentle squeeze. "Don't worry about em or anything they got to say. Not a damn one of em can understand the kind of life you've had to live." When she saw the slight smile crease Emma's lips, she smiled back. "I won't leave you alone."

Just as the wagon pulled up in front of the sheriff's office, Rayne saw Sheriff Kennedy walk out into the street.

"You been readin' my mind, Rayne. I was just plannin' on heading out to your place."

"Needed supplies and wanted to talk with you." Rayne jumped out of the wagon and walked quickly around to help Emma out but the Sheriff got there first.

The sheriff tipped his hat and smiled at Emma as he held out a hand to help her down. "Mornin', Miss Emma. How are ya?"

"I'm doing all right. How about yourself?"

"Doing good." He nodded in Rayne's direction. "How about you?"

"Tell ya what, I'd be doin' a lot better if I knew what the hell is goin' on out at my place."

Tom frowned immediately. "I think you two better come into my office and tell me what is goin' on."

The three went into the sheriff's office.

"I found a section of my fence messed with and I had the strangest feelin' that someone was watching me."

"Did you see any tracks?"

"No, the ground was too hard. When I got back home, MacMillan came up to me warnin' me about Sprigs."

"I know Mac, he ain't got a mean bone in his body. If he warned ya then you best take his words to heart. Now unfortunately, I can't do anything but talk to Sprigs. Keep in mind that you did knock him out and embarrass the man in front of the whole town. Not that he didn't deserve it, but you didn't make him a friend by doin' it. Miss Emma, I'd suggest you keep outta sight for the time bein'."

"I'm not gonna go lookin' for the man but I won't hide from him either. Do you think I'll be safe enough at Rayne's place?" Emma asked.

"I believe so, Emma. She seems to have won over a quite a few folks since knocking Jeremiah on his ass, um, sorry…his backside. I suppose it's fair to say that people took to her quickly, so those close by will be keepin' an eye on her. That bein' said, I reckon you'll be safe enough there."

Emma smiled. "Thank you."

Rayne heard the sheriff's words and wondered if they were true. While she was friendly toward all the people in the town, she hadn't exactly had people knocking down her door to extend their hand in friendship. It was nice to know that people, from the sheriff's viewpoint, were accepting her into their town. Either way, she figured it was good to have others looking out for her.

"Either I'll ride out to the place once a day or I'll have a deputy ride out and check on things," the Sheriff was saying.

"I'd appreciate that, Tom."

"I want to ride up to the rim of the canyon too and look around up there."

"Thank you." Rayne put her hand in the small of Emma's back. "We'd best get goin'."

"If anything else happens, you let me know."

Rayne nodded and guided Emma outside. "Since we're here, I figure we may as well as get more supplies. Maybe more bullets. Just in case."

Chapter Twenty

Back at the canyon, Sprigs rode down the creek toward the spot where he'd loosened the fencing a couple days before. By his calculations, he could start his plan anytime now. He would do it slowly two or three at a time, space it out so he wouldn't draw any attention. Extra head of cattle wouldn't be hard to explain and would go unnoticed. *Hell, by the time she notices anything the creek will have washed out the tracks.* It wasn't until he got closer that he noticed she had repaired the fence.

"God damn it. That bitch found the loosened wire." Now he would have to spend time he didn't have undoing the repair job.

"Wonder where she was goin' in such a rush this morning. Ah shit, you don't suppose she went to tell that ass Kennedy about the fencing do ya, Scout?" he asked his horse. With that thought, he nudged Scout and took off out of the canyon, heading toward his ranch. He was sure it wouldn't be long before the sheriff showed up to question him.

As he rode toward his barn, he saw that indeed the sheriff was there already, talking to his men.

"Hello, Sheriff, how's it goin'?" Sprigs asked as he rode up to the fence.

"Well honestly, Sprigs, it could be a whole lot

better."

"Oh? What's goin' on?"

"You ain't seen any suspicious activity over on the canyon rim, or near the Mathews place have ya?"

"Honestly, I ain't paid a whole lot of attention. I can't recall anything suspicious. Why? What's goin' on?"

"It seems someone's got an eye on Miss Mathews' cattle. She was out ridin' her fence yesterday and found a spot where someone tampered with it."

"Yesterday you say? Now that I think about it, I seem to recall seein' what coulda been a campfire night before last."

"Really? See I find that funny since you were in town that night and I seem to recall that your friends had to carry you home being that Rayne knocked you out cold."

Sprigs felt his face turn red with anger and embarrassment. "God damn it, that bitch had no right hittin' me like that. What are you gonna do about that, Sheriff? Instead of being out here questioning me, you should be out there arresting her for assault."

"Here's the thing, Jeremiah. I'm finding it hard to find anyone that saw exactly what happened. Seems everyone was either playin' cards or too busy jawing with their friends."

"That's bullshit. What about MacMillan or Bigalow?" Sprigs shouted.

"Well now, see here's the problem with that. The only two that are willing to back your story are your hired hands. It seems strange that no one else in the room at the time is willin' to back your story. You kinda see my problem, don't ya?"

"What I see is that you're chicken shit and probably lookin' to put it to that bitch, if ya haven't already."

"Now see here, Sprigs, I do my job and I don't play favorites. If you got a problem with the way I handle things then I suggest you speak with the town folks and see if they agree with you."

"Maybe I'll do just that."

"I'll be waiting." Tom turned and reached for the reins on his horse and swung onto the saddle.

"Boys, thanks for your time, I'll be seen ya." He rode away.

The sheriff rode toward Rayne's ranch so he could do some looking around for himself. Ever since Rayne came to town, he'd been thinking things over and concluded that something had indeed been on Luke Mathews' mind the weeks before his death. He didn't think there was anything suspicious about Luke and Martha's death since it was definitely illness. But there was definitely something going on with the Mathews' place.

When he got to the ranch, he tied his horse to the fence railing and walked around the place. Nothing looked out of place to him but he was determined to look anyway since he just might find something. It wasn't until he walked around the small house that he heard the deep guttural growl of a dog.

The growl stopped him dead in his tracks and brought beads of sweat to his brow. "Oh, hell. Easy there, boy. I ain't here to harm anything, especially you. Tell ya what, why don't I just back on up to my horse and you stay right there and we'll call it good?"

Although he tried to keep his voice calm, he could feel his insides shaking. He stepped backwards. The massive dog tilted his head, his teeth showing the whole time, but just watched and didn't advance.

Once Tom had backed up to his horse, he saw the dog turn and trot back to a spot by the tree in the front yard and lay back down. Tom mounted his horse with a sigh of relief. "That was close." He was thankful that the dog hadn't felt the need to tear him apart.

As his horse trotted along the road, he debated whether he should wait for Rayne or head back to town and arrange a time to look around the place when Rayne was home.

Chapter Twenty-one

Back in town, Rayne and Emma were at the mercantile picking up the things Rayne had ordered and looking for a few things that Emma needed. Rayne figured it was the right thing to do. Since Emma had left with nothing but the clothes on her back, Rayne figured she would need some clothes and personal items. From what Emma had said and what Rayne had gathered from Bessie, she didn't have much in her room at the saloon.

"Come on, I ain't never had anyone to buy for so I'd love buy you some things." Rayne could feel her excitement at the prospect of buying things for Emma. She looked at bolts of fabric and ready-to-wear dresses.

"Rayne no, I really…thank you for your kindness,"

When they left Gillum's Mercantile, their arms were loaded with packages. The items that Rayne had ordered the day before last were already packed in the wagon. Rayne's determination to make the little house a home was even stronger than ever. Before Emma, it was nice to go back to the house after a hard day's work. After last night, when she rode up to the house and saw a light glowing in the window, she felt a warmth that was stronger than she had ever felt before.

She knew it was because of the woman that walked beside her now.

Today, she couldn't wait to get back and start constructing a nicer table and fixing up the small house. She had even bought new curtains for the rooms. Before, she had been happy with just a blanket to tack up at night. Things had changed.

As Rayne took the packages and finished loading up the wagon, she smiled a smile that went clear to her heart. It melted the icy coldness in her eyes that had built a home there lately.

"You look happy, Rayne. What happened to put that shine in your eyes?" Emma asked.

"I bought some curtains for the house, and some finishing supplies for the new table I'm makin'. Yeah, I suppose I am real happy,"

Emma flashed a smile of her own. "I like it when you smile like that."

Rayne blushed at the comment and couldn't stop another genuine smiled from crossing her face. She helped Emma up onto the wagon seat and climbed on as well, ready to head back to their home.

Wait, when did it become our *home?*

Rayne liked that thought. She was already thinking of what she could do to make Emma more comfortable and more at home. *Jesus, Rayne, you ain't looking for nothin but heartache thinkin' that way.*

"So, is there anything else you need?" Rayne asked.

"Oh, I think I have enough, thank you." Emma replied. "Rayne, I don't know how to thank you or let alone know how I'm going to repay you."

"Don't worry about it, Em. Way I figure it, I'll get fat with you cooking for me. Hell, that would be good enough." Rayne stole a look out of the corner of her eye and saw the pink on Emma's cheeks. *God, she is beautiful,* she thought. The way the bright sunshine made Emma's hair shine took Rayne's breath away.

"Have you given much thought about what you're gonna do? Not that you have to or anything. I mean you're welcome to stay as long as you'd like. In fact, you'd be doin' me a favor." Rayne, realizing what she just said, felt her cheeks heat up.

"What do you mean? I'd be doin' you a favor? How?"

"Well, honestly. I hate my cookin'and most of the time I just eat a slice of bread for dinner or lunch. My coffee tastes like mud, and me makin' a pie…you gotta be kiddin'. Last night's dinner was amazing and I honestly didn't realize I had the things to make a cobbler in my root cellar, course I never bothered to look in much less find it so I suppose that coulda been part of my problem. But if you keep making me meals like that, I got no problem with you stayin' for as long as you like."

"What if I had plans on movin' on to another town?" Emma asked. "Perhaps I have some distant relative, or friends livin' elsewhere?"

"If you have plans then by all means you should go ahead with them. However, I'd say first off that if you had some distant relative, I highly doubt that you would have spent your life in a saloon bein' cared for by whores." Rayne dared not look at Emma and stared straight ahead.

"Excuse me, but you have no idea about my life or those that raised me. All you have is gossip from a bunch of old women with nothing better to do than speak behind other's backs. My folks died leaving me alone and helpless. I was only one year old and an orphan. Fern took me and made sure that I knew how to take care of myself. So did all the other girls at the saloon."

Emma's jaw clenched. "Did you or anyone in this damned town for one second take into account that Fern and all the other girls did what they had so they could support themselves in order to survive? They didn't have the luxury of relatives leaving them a ranch and money."

Emma continued blasting at Rayne. "Did any one of them offer a single ounce of compassion to them or me? No, honestly the only one in this town who never looked down at us was Bessie." Emma swiped at the tears of anger that fell from her eyes.

"I'm sorry, Em. I didn't mean to talk bad about Fern or the others. Hell, I know they done what they needed to do. All's I mean was if you had family, you'd have been raised by them not the ladies at the saloon."

"Oh, so all of a sudden they are *ladies*?

"Goddamn it, Em. Stop it. You know damn well I ain't never made a derogatory remark about you or any of them girls at Hank's place. So I'd appreciate it if you'd stop making assumptions about what I'm sayin'."

The rest of the ride back to the ranch was spent in silence. Rayne didn't mean anything by what she had said and was downright mad that Emma assumed that she had.

Chapter Twenty-two

Emma thought about her reaction to Rayne's words.

Did I overreact? Rayne has no reason to assume I don't have family elsewhere.

But Rayne was right. If she had family, there is no way they'd let her be raised in a house of prostitutes. And not once had she heard Rayne make any comments about the women and how they made their living.

In fact, she stood up for me when it mattered. So why did I fly off the handle like that?

The only conclusion Emma could come up with—she didn't want Rayne to think less of her, or any of the women at the saloon.

Why it matters so much to me what Rayne thinks is a mystery to me, she thought.

As the wagon pulled into the yard of the small ranch, the big black dog appeared with his tail wagging. His dark gaze was on the women as Rayne helped Emma down. Lucifer ambled up to Emma and pushed his head under her hand. Emma scratched the top of Lucifer's head, which seemed to satisfy him, and he ambled back to his spot under the tree.

Rayne unloaded the items that went into the house and Emma carried them inside

"That should do it for the house stuff." Rayne shrugged. "I'm gonna get the wood and rest of the supplies and put them in the barn."

"Okay, I'll take care of the things in the house and start makin' dinner."

Rayne nodded and pulled several pieces of wood out of the wagon and settled them on her shoulder. Once it all was where it belonged, she looked around with satisfaction. This place was hers. She didn't have to work till her back ached and she had inches of dirt on her for someone else's benefit. In her mind, that made all the difference in the world.

With a sigh of happiness, she climbed up the ladder to the hayloft and began pitching straw down. Lucifer trotted in a few minutes later and instantly his hackles went up. He bared his teeth and with his head down, flew at a wolf that had been hiding in a corner of the barn. Startled by the growling, Rayne took a step back. Her foot hit the edge of the loft and before she could do anything, she and the pitchfork were flying down ten feet onto the hard ground below. The dog and the wolf were sailing through the air in combat. The two animals landed a few feet away from Rayne who was trying to reach for her gun before everything went black.

✝

A gunshot brought Emma running out of the house. Her heart dropped when she saw Rayne on the ground and the back of a man holding a gun. Grabbing the first thing she could, she ran up behind the man and swung as hard as she could.

The blow of the broom handle hit the shoulder blade of the man who instantly spun around and blocked Emma's next swing.

"Hey, hold on there. Damn it, Emma, stop fightin' me." Tom yelled as he blocked another swing of the broom.

"You shot Rayne. Why?" Emma couldn't stop her tears.

"I shot the damn wolf, not Rayne." The sheriff rushed over to Rayne who lay on the ground not moving.

All Emma could see or feel was that she was living through yet another nightmare. She believed deep in her heart that she had lived many lifetimes losing the woman she loved. Somehow she knew that woman was Rayne. Once she came to the realization that Rayne wasn't dead, she rushed to her side.

"Is she all right?" She knelt beside the sheriff.

"She's breathing and it don't feel like there's anything broke. She has one hell of a knot on her head though." He gently felt the back of the Rayne's head again. "Go grab a cold cloth."

Emma rushed back to the small house and soon came back with a wet cloth, which she applied to the unconscious woman.

✝

Rayne slowly regained consciousness and sat up immediately then held her head. "Everything is spinning."

"Whoa there, not too fast, Rayne. Can ya tell me what happened?"

"Ouch, damn that hurts." Rayne reached back and touched the bump on her head. "I think Lucifer was tryin' to save me. I was cleaning out the loft and heard Lucifer growling and when I looked, that wolf was attackin' him. Shit, did Lucifer get bit or scratched?" Rayne asked as she tried to rise to check on the dog.

"I don't know. I don't believe it's somethin' we should wait to find out." The sheriff stood and pointed his forty-five at the animal.

"*No.* Don't you dare shoot him," Rayne hollered as she gripped her aching head.

"What?" Tom looked at Emma and raised his eyebrows.

"Tom, he was saving my life. I can't just let you shoot him. Let's give him a chance. We'll lock him up and see if he develops signs of mad dog disease."

Rayne looked at Emma. "You won't get near him is that understood? I've seen an animal with the disease and it ain't pretty.

Emma shook her head. "Rayne, this isn't a good idea. Look at that wolf, there is foam on her mouth. She sure as heck had rabies. I don't think it's a good idea to take a wait and see attitude with demon dog here."

"Look, he's my dog. I'll shoot him if need be but I'm gonna give him a chance." She stood and walked shakily toward the big black dog

"Damn it, Rayne…." Tom tried to grab Rayne's arm.

"Lucifer, come on." Once Lucifer was following her, Rayne walked to a smaller out building and opened the door. "Inside." The big dog walked in with his head down. He obviously thought he was being punished.

"I just can't take the chance, Lucifer. Too many lives are at stake here. I'll be back to check on you. I'll take care of ya." Rayne tried to explain as she closed the door.

Rayne walked away from the dog and the building with a sinking feeling in her stomach. She looked up and saw that Tom was taking care of the wolf. With a good look at the wolf's carcass, she saw that it had indeed been foaming at the mouth.

Tom wrapped the wolf's body in a burlap bag he found in the barn.

Rayne approached the sheriff.

"I'll be back to check on you, Rayne, I need to bury this poor animal."

"Tom, be careful please," Emma said. "Rayne, you come in and lay down. The sheriff will be back…won't you, Tom? I'll fix us a nice meal. It's the least I can do for you."

"Yup, I'll be back. I need to talk to you two about the troubles you've had here."

"What'd you find, Tom?" Rayne asked.

Emma looked at Rayne and saw her eyes close. "How's the pain?"

"It feels like a hammer is hitting against my skull. I'm dizzy and my stomach doesn't feel too good." She rubbed her head. "God, I hate how I feel right now."

"We can do it later, Rayne. Right now you need to lie down." Tom rushed to Rayne's side just in time to catch her as her legs gave out from under her. Tom carried Rayne toward the house as Emma rushed ahead to open the door.

Emma opened the bedroom door. "Put her down on the bed and I'll take care of her."

Once Tom laid Rayne on the bed, Emma became a whirlwind of activity by rushing to the kitchen for cold water, and whatever else she needed to get for the unconscious woman.

"Look, I'm gonna take care of the wolf and then head into town to fetch Doc Adams. I wanna make sure that Rayne is all right."

"Do you think she's hurt badly?" Emma wrung her hands and looked at Rayne.

"Just wanna make sure, Emma. She took a bad tumble outta that barn loft. I was honestly surprised that she can feel her legs, let alone walk. Right now, I'd just feel better if the Doc checked her over."

Tipping his hat, Tom went back the way he came in.

†

Tom loaded the wrapped up body of the wolf on his horse behind the saddle and rode off toward town. He stopped at his home and grabbed a shovel before going to the doc's place.

Doc Adams eyed the sheriff and nodded at his saddle. "What's going on, Tom."

"Think I shot a mad dog wolf over at the Mathews' place. Rayne took a tumble off the hay loft and isn't looking good.

"Let me get my bag."

As soon as Doc Adams was ready, they mounted their horses.

"We need to stop on the way and bury the wolf."

"I'd like to get a good look at the animal."

"Yup, you can do that when we find a good spot to bury it."

Tom pointed to a secluded area and guided his horse toward it. "This'll do."

Once the wolf was on the ground, Doc Adams squatted down and pulled back the burlap. "Yup, that sure is rabies. Ya sure the Mathews woman didn't get bit?"

"Yeah, she didn't have any scratches or bites that could have come from the animal. To me it looked like Rayne's dog threw himself in the wolf's way."

"All right. Let's get this poor animal buried and get out to the Mathews place."

It was early evening when the two men rode up to Rayne's place. Hearing the dog from the closed building barking up a storm, Emma went out to greet them.

"Miss Emma, it's good to see ya again. Sorry I

haven't had a chance to give my condolences to ya. I know you was real close to Fern."

"I understand, Doctor Adams, and thank you."

"For what child?" Confusion was clear on his face.

"For taking care of Fern. For making sure she was at least comfortable and not alone when she passed on."

"Honestly, Emma, I don't believe she knew what happened. Whatever that man did to her, she was out long before he left her. She didn't regain consciousness."

With the fresh gleam of tears brimming in her eyes, Emma cleared her throat. "Come on in. I expect you're wanting to take a look at Rayne. She has been awake off and on and drank a little tea but she doesn't want to eat anything. She keeps saying her head feels like it wants to explode." Emma could feel her insides shaking as she worried about Rayne. "When you're done taking a look at her I got supper ready for both of you."

Together the three walked into the house and Emma showed the doc to the bedroom, where they found Rayne sitting on the edge of the bed ready to stand up.

"Just where do you think you're goin'?" Emma asked in a stern, motherly voice.

"Well, I heard Lucifer barking and I was gonna go check on him."

"Oh, lord. You will do no such thing. Now you lay yourself right back down on that bed. Doc Adams is here to see you."

"I don't need to see the doc..."

"Oh, yes you do. He took the time to ride all the way out here so the least you can do is be civil. Now lie back down and don't argue with me."

Both men standing in the doorway smirked.

Tom and Emma walked out to the living area of the house, leaving the doctor and Rayne alone.

"Can I get you something to drink?" Emma offered.

"No. I'm good."

"It's been quite a day, hasn't it?" Emma said.

"Yup it has. Doc looked at the wolf and said it was rabid."

"I hate to see Lucifer locked up...but it's for the best."

They sat in companionable silence until they heard the door to the bedroom open.

The doc came out of the bedroom followed by Rayne who looked a tad pale.

"Where do you think you're going?" Emma asked as she rushed over to the woman.

"Thought I'd go to my chair and sit out here, why?"

"Doc, is that all right? Should she be up and around already?" Emma asked.

"I'll tell ya what, if you can keep this young woman down, go right on ahead. As far as she is concerned, she is fine and medically speaking, I have to caution her to take things slow, but I see no reason for her to remain in bed." He turned to Rayne. "That is as long as you remember to take it easy."

"I will. I promise, but damn it, I got crops and cattle to tend to. I can't just lie around here."

"We'll see to your animals for a few days, Rayne." Tom knew the men in nearby ranches would be willing to help out and he knew for sure that he would ride out a couple of times a day to see to the animals.

"Tom, that's too much to ask of you all," Rayne said.

"Not at all. I know you don't see it or even understand it right now, but everyone in this town had a special place in their hearts for Luke and Martha. Bein' their kin…well, that means we look out for you as well. And, no one is gonna come out and say it but, there a few that figure ya done right by Miss Emma here. You stood up for her when there was no one else. Ya took her in and well, circumstances bein' what they are…well…it's the least we can do. I don't think I'm talkin' outta turn here either. Do you, Doc?"

"Not at all. I, for one, always worried about Emma. That saloon ain't no place for a young woman such as her. With Fern not around to stand up or take care of this youngun…just hated to think of what she woulda ended up being. I hope ya don't just throw her to the wolves, if ya know what I mean," Doc Adams said. "You are a Godsend for Emma and I pray that you will see to Emma's safekeeping."

Rayne looked from the Doc to Tom who was nodding his agreement. "Even with my head pounding, I know there is no way in this world that I'd turn my back on Emma."

Emma, not knowing what to do or say, excused herself. "I need to check on supper."

In the kitchen, Emma leaned against the counter and recalled all the dreams she had had about a tall, dark-haired woman. How many times in her dreams, had she looked at the beautiful woman and wondered if it would be the last time. Would she see her again in that particular lifetime? She didn't know but she had felt it again earlier that afternoon. She hated that feeling, and she knew it wasn't dreams, she knew they were memories of previous lives with Rayne. Emma regained her composure and walked back into the sitting room.

"Supper is ready."

As the three people stood, Emma walked to Rayne, helped her to her feet, and with her arm around Rayne's waist, walked with her to the small dining area where she helped her to her chair.

"Something sure smells good," Tom said as he pulled Emma's chair out for her.

"It sure does," Doc chimed in as he sat down.

In front of them on the table sat golden-roasted chicken, mashed potatoes and gravy, biscuits and some green beans.

"Thank you. Please help yourselves. Here, Rayne, let me get you a plate." Emma reached for Rayne's plate.

Before Rayne could say anything, a plate sat in front of her with a little of everything. "Even with the headache, it smells wonderful. I can't remember ever smelling anything so mouthwatering."

For a few minutes, the only sounds were the clanking of silverware on plates and bowls as they served themselves.

After a few bites, Rayne looked at the sheriff. "Tom, I wanna thank you for coming around when ya did. That wolf would have had me for lunch for sure."

"I'm glad I was here," Tom replied.

"So, I know you weren't just out ridin' around. What brought you by?"

"This can wait until you're feelin' better, Rayne."

"It's just a headache, right, Doc? I can talk, right?"

"Well, there's nothing broken and I still think you should be in bed resting. I did tell you I think ya rang your bell pretty good."

"Things need to be done around here and I ain't got time to lounge around in bed, Doc."

"I understand, and I do believe Tom here has offered the help of your neighbors as well as his own. I know I am tad handy with plow. Between all of us, we can have your ranch in tiptop shape in no time, and I ain't askin' ya to take a year off. For Pete's sake, just sayin' take a day or two to make sure you're all right is all I'm askin'."

"Rayne, I think you should listen to the doctor. He knows what he is talking about," Emma said.

"You feel the same way, Tom?"

"Sorry, but, yeah, I do."

"Tom, what would you do if it were your place and you was bein' told to take it easy?" Rayne asked.

"I imagine I'd feel like you are at the moment, but, I'd also look at all the friends I have willin' to see to it that I don't lose anything. Like I said, I know you ain't seen it, but folks around here take care of their own and, well, like it or not, you're one of us. You're Luke and Martha's kin, ya took Emma here in when she needed it, and hell, ya even took in that damn demon dog out there. That tells us all there's a good heart in ya. Come on, let us help you."

"Oh, all right…but just for a few days. But I ain't layin' around like some princess, I'll do what I can and when I start to feelin' bad I'll come back in for a bit."

"That sounds fair. Don't you think sheriff? Doc?" Emma smiled.

"Sure does." Tom replied.

Doc Adams nodded in agreement.

"Now how about I clear these dishes and bring out some coffee?" Emma said as she stood.

Doc Adams stood as well and began helping Emma clear the dishes.

"Rayne, I came by earlier to tell ya that I spoke with Sprigs this morning. Says he ain't been around and that he ain't seen nothing strange. Unless you count the campfire, he says he seen night before last. I did come by earlier to talk with ya, but met old Lucifer instead. He don't seem to take kindly to folks walkin' around the place when you ain't here." Tom chuckled.

"Yeah, he's kinda funny that way. Did you head up to the rim to see about that campfire?" Rayne gave her head a small shake. "Tryin' to clear the cobwebs."

"Give it time. In answer to your question, no, I

didn't. After stopping here, I decided I didn't want that dog following me and leaving me in bits up there. I figured I'd come back and see if you wanted to go up with me…instead I see you come flyin' outta that loft. Think you took twenty years off my life."

"Sorry about that, Sheriff. Though I am glad you came by when ya did." Rayne said.

"Here we go, coffee and cake." Emma walked into the dining area with Doc Adams following her holding the cake.

"Emma, you didn't have to go through all this trouble." Tom's eyes looked at the chocolate cake and he licked his lips. "That cake sure looks good."

"It was my pleasure, Tom. After all, you did save Rayne's life."

"Oh, I don't know about that. I think Lucifer had that all covered before I rode up."

"Yeah, well, you're the one who shot the wolf. I think that wolf wanted to have him for dinner. Speaking of which, I do need to go check on him. Give him water and some food." Rayne said as she made to stand up.

"You just sit down, Rayne. I'll see to him." Emma placed a slice of cake in front of her.

"You stay the hell away from him, you hear me." Rayne pushed the chair back and stood up fast.

Tom and Emma were right there to catch her before she fell. As Emma picked up the chair that had fallen, Tom held her steady.

"Do not speak to me in that tone, Rayne Mathews," Emma scolded.

"Sorry I didn't mean to, but that dog is a danger right now and I won't have you near him. I'll tend to him."

"But you're in no condition to tend to him yourself right now," Emma argued.

"Emma, if you go near him I swear to, God, I'll…"

"You'll do what?" Emma eyes flashed with a spark of anger.

"Emma, don't you understand? If he was bit he could have been infected… I can't take that chance," Rayne said.

"Fine, but he has to eat too. How are you going to manage that? You look like you're about to fall over."

Rayne was sweating by the time she finally made it to the bed. She fell into the soft mattress and passed out cold.

Chapter Twenty-three

With the help of her the town men and Emma, Rayne's ranch was running smoothly. Each morning the animals were fed, and while everyone hollered about it, it was Rayne who fed Lucifer. She felt it was the least she could do since she was the one locking him up. Under no circumstance would she risk injury to Em or to any of the others. Yet it was a battle with the feisty blonde each time Rayne stood to go out to feed Lucifer. Each morning and each evening, she looked for signs of rabies and to her relief each time she found nothing.

By the time a couple of weeks had passed, Rayne was up and around and feeling back to normal. She sensed that Emma was always watching her to make sure she was indeed as fine as she claimed to be and that made her feel happy. Rayne had settled into a relaxed comfortable pattern of domestic life.

Emma was up each morning before her and had coffee ready by the time Rayne walked out of the bedroom and headed out to feed the horses and chickens. When she came back in, Emma had breakfast on the table with a steaming cup of fresh coffee ready.

Each morning when Rayne felt Emma get out of bed, she enjoyed the sound of her bustling around in the kitchen as she put coffee on the small iron holder.

At first, it took her some time before she was able to follow her quickly out of bed. For the first week, all Rayne heard was, *No sit yourself right there and don't worry about the animals, I will get to them.* Usually, by the time, the coffee was ready, either Doc or Tom would be there, tossing oats and hay to the horses and cracked corn to the chickens. By the time they were done, Emma had a plate for them sitting on the table along with coffee and wouldn't take no for an answer from them when they would say they just stopped by. If they had to leave, Emma would wrap up the biscuits and bacon to send with them.

One such morning, Rayne was sitting t the table with Doc and Tom while Emma insisted on feeding the chickens. Rayne only shook her head as Emma left them alone.

"Ya know, Rayne, Emma is a sweet girl and I am sure glad you rescued her from that saloon. Ever since her folks died and Fern took over her care I've worried about her. That was no life for her." Doc pointed his fork at Rayne. "Now you listen to me." He narrowed his eyes. "You need someone to take care of you and she needs a home."

"You two are a good match," Tom added. "You couldn't ask for a better person than Emma."

Rayne remained still just sitting there listening to the two men as her heart nodded in agreement.

A few weeks after Rayne recovered and Doc had given her the go ahead, she was back on Apache, riding fence. As she looked out at her land, the sight of the small herd, her house that sat off in the distance, the green meadow, and the stream that flowed through it all made her feel calm—something she hadn't felt in a very long time. A sense of belonging flowed through her.

The slight breeze that blew around her and the scent of the wildflowers in the air mixed with the warmth of the sun gave her such a blessed feeling. She smiled at the realization that she was home. This right here was everything she had wished for, right down to the woman currently in her kitchen fixing lunch.

With a smile, she nudged the bay and headed toward home.

When Rayne walked inside the house, she headed straight to the kitchen.

"Hey, you're in early. Good thing I put the chicken to fry earlier."

"Smells great, is it about done?"

"It is. I actually have it in the Dutch oven to keep warm. Are you hungry now? I can fry up some potatoes real fast if you are."

"Why don't we throw the chicken in a basket along with some apples and head on down to the creek?" Rayne leaned back against the door jam. "It's a beautiful day, would be a shame to let it go to waste."

"Oh, don't be silly. I have the house to clean, laundry to do…." Emma said.

Rayne let a slow smile cross her face.

"Are you serious? You aren't just teasing me are you?"

"Sure, I'm serious. Come on, what are you waitin'

for? If you take any more time, the afternoon'll be gone." Rayne walked over to the storage room and fetched a small basket.

"Here, I'll get that." Emma reached for the basket and began placing towels in it before she pulled out the chicken from the oven.

With a big smile, Rayne went into the bedroom and grabbed a blanket, went back outside, and strapped it to the back of the saddle that sat on Apache. She reached for her canteen, went to the water barrel, and filled it with cold water before replacing it on the saddle beside her rifle. She went back into the house to get Emma and the basket of chicken.

Emma grabbed her sunbonnet and followed Rayne out the door.

Rayne put her foot in the stirrup and pushed off and up onto the bay. She reached for the basket, and hooked it to the saddle horn. She then reached out for Emma and helped her mount the horse behind her. With Emma's arms wrapped around her waist, Rayne guided Apache toward the meadow and a shady spot by the creek.

†

Emma smelled the fresh wildflowers as the warm sun shone down on her. She was the happiest she had ever been, of that she was sure. In the few short weeks that she had lived with Rayne, she knew Rayne was everything she had ever dreamed of... and exactly who she dreamed of.

As they rode up to the spot where Rayne chose to stop, Emma gasped. As Rayne helped her off the horse, she looked around and smiled. Emma was in awe at the beauty of the spot

Rayne dismounted, untied the blanket, grabbed the basket, and the canteen while Emma walked around just breathing in the scent of nature and listening to the birds and the sound of the water trickling softly over the rocks, making its way to who knew where.

"Do you like it?" Rayne walked up behind Emma and wrapped her arms around her, and placed her chin against Emma's head.

"It's beautiful, Rayne. So quiet and peaceful."

"Yeah, that it is."

"Do you come here often?" Emma asked.

"No, I don't…haven't had the time. I found it when I first got here but then…well, things started happening and I got busy. Come on, let's spread out the blanket."

Rayne reached for Emma's hand and they walked to a spot where she had dropped the blanket, the chicken, and the canteen.

Together they spread out the blanket, sat down, and opened the basket.

After the meal of still-warm chicken, they lay on the blanket and looked up at the clouds, pointing out shapes. Their hands brushed and touched whenever possible. With the passing of the afternoon, their touches lasted longer and became bolder.

With a sigh of regret, Emma smiled at Rayne. "This has been lovely. Thank you."

"I'm happy you liked it. It is getting close to the time when the animals need feeding and bedding down."

"It's been a wonderful afternoon, one I'll never forget, Rayne. I hope we do this again soon."

Rayne let out contented sigh. "Me too." They packed everything up and she mounted Apache holding out her hand for Emma. Once Emma was settled behind her, Rayne nudged the horse toward home.

As they rode back to the homestead, Emma had her arms around Rayne's waist with her head resting against the solid, warm back. She knew she belonged with Rayne and God help her, it was where she would stay.

Chapter Twenty-four

The yard was quiet when they rode in, and instantly Rayne felt something was wrong. Her eyes carefully took in everything, and stopped as she caught sight of the building that housed Lucifer. She stopped Apache instantly and pulled her long legs over the saddle, careful not to knock Emma down. Without hesitation, she reached up, pulled the blonde off the horse.

"Stay put," Rayne told Emma before running to the building.

The door to the shed stood open and Rayne heard no sound coming from inside. Slowly, before making her way inside, she drew the forty-five that was strapped to her hip. The coppery smell of blood reached her nose and when her eyes adjusted, she caught sight of the lifeless body of the black dog. With her chest heaving, she stumbled back, turned away, and headed for the back of the building before she lost the contents of her stomach.

"Rayne what is going on?" Emma called out.

"Stay where you are, Emma." Rayne's voice brooked no argument.

Emma stayed put.

Rayne steeled her emotions and came around the building

Emma started walking toward Rayne and stopped

suddenly. "Rayne, are you all right?"

"Yeah, though I think we are heading to town again. I'll saddle up Delilah. Stay away from that building. Do you understand me?"

"Rayne, what happened? Where's Lucifer?"

"I…we don't have time for me to tell you…I need to get Delilah saddled." Rayne walked toward the barn.

Emma went toward the shed and walked inside.

The only thing Rayne heard was the piercing scream coming from Emma, and she was out of the barn like a lightning bolt. Not seeing Emma, she ran to the shed where she found Emma standing with her hands over her mouth.

"Em, Emma, look at me, come on, let's get out of here. No…stay with me. Shit." Rayne caught Emma in her arms before she slumped to the ground. Picking up the beautiful blonde, she walked directly to the house, and with her foot kicked open the door. She walked to the sofa and gently placed Emma down. She stroked her cheek before she turned on her heel and went into the bedroom for a washcloth from the washbasin on the dresser. As she kneeled beside Emma, she tenderly placed the cold cloth on her forehead.

With her voice low and soft, Rayne said, "Come on, baby, it's okay. Open your eyes. I swear I won't let anything happen to you. I know I've let you down before but not this time. I've learned my lesson. You are all that matters. Wake up, honey."

"What…Oh, God, Rayne, what happened?" Emma regained consciousness and her arms reached for

Rayne.

"I don't know, baby, I don't know. But I do know we need to get to Tom's as quick as we can. Do you think you can ride?"

"Yes, I think I can. Can we go now please?" Emma answered in a shaky voice.

Rayne walked behind Emma, already deciding that she would not be riding Delilah to town. She knew Emma had very little experience riding a horse on her own and didn't have the strength to stay on the animal. She reached for the horse and tethered her to the closest post. Emma looked at her questioningly. "You're riding with me. I don't think you have the strength to ride alone. I won't leave you here alone."

"Rayne, I'll be fine on Delilah."

"Well maybe, but ever consider I might need you with me and I was just looking for an excuse?" Rayne replied shakily.

"All right," Emma said. "Let's get going before it gets much later. The sooner we see Tom, the sooner we find out who did that to Lucifer."

"That's my girl." Rayne smiled a halfhearted smile. She helped Emma up onto Apache once more and got on behind her this time. With the reins in hand and Emma wrapped in the circle of her arms, Rayne spurred the large bay into a run.

Chapter Twenty-five

Once Tom finished looking around Rayne's place, he and Rayne buried Lucifer.

Tom pushed his hat back on his head and rubbed his hand over the stubble on his chin. "Don't know who would do this to your dog, Rayne. You have my word I will do all I can to find out."

"Thanks, Tom, I appreciate it."

"I don't have a good feelin' about this." Tom shook his head as he mounted his horse. "I guess I'd better head back to town. You and Emma goin' to be okay?"

"We'll be fine." Rayne nodded and slapped the horse's hindquarter and watched as the sheriff moved up the road before she headed into the house.

Rayne walked inside and dropped into the nearest chair. She felt extremely guilty, and had experienced that feeling the entire ride into and back from town. She had a huge sense of relief that they hadn't been home when whoever it was paid them a visit. She also had a deep sense of sorrow. She wondered if she could have saved Lucifer's life, or at least made his death not so callous. She knew from looking at Lucifer's body, that he had suffered and that his death had been painful and drawn out. She also knew that had they been home, that could have very well happened to them. A very angry person was behind the killing and that thought both scared and worried her.

"Rayne."

The soft voice broke into Rayne's weary thoughts.

"Come eat something."

"I'm not very hungry," she answered quietly.

"I know, but you have to at least try, Rayne," Emma replied. "It's not much, just some soup and biscuits."

Rayne sighed, and tiredly stood.

Emma took hold of her hand and they walked into the kitchen.

Rayne sat down and looked at Emma who sat across from her. She tried to smile, just as Emma did, but both finally just gave up and half-heartedly ate.

As Emma cleaned up the kitchen, Rayne stepped outside for some fresh air.

Rayne hadn't been outside long when she heard the squeak of the door and felt a soft warm hand on her shoulder. She turned and they wrapped their arms around one another in mutual need.

"Long evening…" Emma said.

"Yup, it has been. I'm sorry you saw Lucifer like that. I shoulda told you to go inside or somethin'."

"It's not your fault. You told me to stay put and I chose not to listen." Emma tightened her arms around Rayne.

Before Rayne knew what she was doing, she softly placed a kiss on the top of Emma's head. She breathed in the sweet smell of the soap Emma had washed her hair with earlier that morning.

Emma slowly lifted her head with eyes searching Rayne's face.

Rayne slowly lowered her face and her lips gently touched those of Emma. At first, it was a simple brush of their lips, then another and yet another. Before either knew, Rayne's tongue was slowly parting Emma's warm, welcoming lips.

As quickly as she had started it, Rayne ended it.

Emma stepped back and, casting her eyes downward, walked into the house.

Oh, God, what did I just do, what must she think. She must think I'm some kind of sick deviant, Rayne thought with a lurch of horror.

†

Emma didn't realize it was Rayne who kissed her. Confused by her own actions, Emma heard the door close behind her. It was only then that she realized that Rayne was standing behind her. She leaned into the lips nuzzling her neck and the hands gently resting on her hips. Only when she heard a soft moan did she even realize that it was coming from her throat. She turned into Rayne's arms and met her kiss with one as hard and fiery as the one Rayne was giving her.

With the fire burning hotter, the two worked at removing layers of clothing as they moved to the bedroom. Naked, they landed on the bed as their mouths and fingers explored one another.

†

Rayne couldn't recall anyone tasting as sweet and feeling as soft as Emma did, and she was lost in the sensations. The kisses were fiery and added to the ache that had developed in her and, she suspected, in Emma too.

Rayne's hands roamed over the soft warm body that lay under her. Feeling it created a need inside her that she had not felt as strongly before Emma. Slowly her mouth moved to Emma's neck kissing and gently nipping as her hand moved to cup a full breast. Her thumb brushing over the nipple caused it to become hard and Emma took in a quick breath. Rayne moved her mouth down and found the nipple. She gently flicked her tongue over it, back and forth, alternating between gentle and hard. She could feel the need in Emma when her hand moved to hold Rayne's head in place.

Rayne's hand made its way to the juncture of Emma's legs and felt the slick wetness that she was creating. Her fingers began to stroke Emma's pink nub gently. With Emma breathing harder and faster, Rayne continued to stroke and suck on the nipple, before slowly sliding a finger into Emma's wet center. Deeper and deeper she went, trying to keep things slow but failing as Emma brought her hips up, urging her to push her fingers deeper. Before Rayne realized it, a rhythm was set, one that would quickly drive Emma over the edge.

It seemed to Rayne that she had just shut her eyes when the sun dawned. With a contented sigh, she looked at Emma whose head was resting on her shoulder. This feeling of complete joy and happiness was what she had searched for her whole life.

Where do we go from here, though?

It was hard being a female rancher and farmer of the Rocking M Ranch. As far as she could tell, the people of Willow Springs accepted her and didn't give her much trouble. She realized how lucky she was in that respect for they could have made her life much more difficult. The only real trouble with anyone around was with Sprigs and whoever tore up her home, tried to rustle her cattle, and had killed her dog. Sprig, maybe?

The image of Lucifer lying in a pool of blood brought her back down to earth.

"What's on your mind, Rayne? You seem a million miles away."

Rayne heard the soft voice and turned her head. "Mmm…just thinking how nice this is." She smiled at Emma and let out a contented breath.

"Oh, I don't think so. A frown isn't usually symbolic of happiness." Emma's fingers began to brush across Rayne's taut stomach.

"God, woman, you make it difficult to think." Rayne captured Emma's hand. "And you are insatiable as well. As much as I'd like to stay and fix that, I unfortunately have livestock to tend to."

She grinned. "Though I just might come back here when I'm done and at least attempt to fix your problem."

Rayne scampered out of bed just as Emma was about to swat her. She reached for her pants and was putting them on when she saw Emma stretching. The blankets were slipping down and Rayne could see the swell of Emma's perfectly formed breasts. With a groan, Rayne forced her eyes away as she reached for her shirt, put it on, gave Emma one last glance, and headed out to the other room

Emma's rich laugher followed her all the way out the door.

With a smile on her face and that lingering sense of finally belonging, Rayne went about her morning chores. She whistled a tune as she fed the horses and the chickens before she raked out the stalls in the barn. She felt so happy she gave both Apache and Delilah an extra bucket of oats. A sense of sorrow hit her when she looked out to where Lucifer always laid in the morning sun.

"Goddamn it!" Her eyes went to the building where Lucifer had lived the last few weeks of his life. She ached, knowing that she had almost decided that he was free of rabies and was going to let him out. "Lucifer, I swear I'll find who did that to ya."

Rayne shook away her sad thoughts and continued with her work, smiling when she thought of Emma and the night they had spent together.

Chapter Twenty-six

With a smile she couldn't stop, Emma dressed and went to the kitchen to start the coffee before making bacon, eggs, and biscuits. Last night had worked up an appetite. At least she knew it had for her. She hadn't felt like this before. There was an excitement shaking deep inside her and a sense of completeness that until now had only been in her dreams. As she cooked the meal, her mind drifted back in time where there was just an enclosed hut and an opening in the thatched roof for the smoke to flow through....

The air outside was chilled, and the rolling hills had a blanket of mist covering them. The sounds of animals baying for food and the deep throaty voice of her lover as she spoke to them floated to her ears. With a smile, she prepared for the day ahead. Life was hard and the work was even harder, but she was happy because together with the woman she loved, they were carving out a life to themselves. Rae, tanned from the sun, looked magnificent. Her hair held silver streaks intertwined with the dark brown. Her frame was lean and muscular, hands rough from working the land, and without a doubt the woman had the biggest heart in the Highlands. Of course, she also held a very strong sense of right and wrong and when crossed or angered, not even the biggest man was willing to step in.

"What ye thinkin, me love."

Emma heard the voice come from behind her. Her heart skipped a few beats upon hearing the rich, thick Scot-accented voice that belonged to Rae.

"Mm, I was thinkin' it was about time for ye to come eat."

"Aye, that it be, and ta be honest with ye, I'm famished." Rae had a wicked smile as her arms went around Em and her lips descended on the soft lips in hunger.

It was the door closing softly that brought Emma out of her thoughts. When she looked up and saw Rayne walk into the kitchen, her heart skipped a beat just as it had in her dreams.

"What's the smile all about?" Rayne asked as the edges of her lips tugged into a similar smile of her own.

"I was just thinkin' about last night and this mornin'," Emma replied.

"Ah, and were you thinkin' anythin' in particular?"

"Mmm, maybe. But your breakfast is getting cold."

"Oh, we can't have that." Rayne laughed as she sat down and began eating. After just a few bites, she suddenly mumbled something and excused herself.

Emma, who was busy getting food on her own plate felt both surprised and uncomfortable.

In the barn Rayne paced, embarrassment and anger surging through her. How could she have been so stupid? Did she honestly believe that the beautiful blonde woman inside her house could actually have been happy with the way she had forced herself on her last night?

Just because she had worked in a saloon didn't mean she would... Jesus Christ, Rayne, she told you that son of a bitch Sprigs had been her first, what in the hell makes you think she even welcomed your touch? She isn't a whore for Christ's sake.

With her mood growing darker by the minute, Rayne went to work mucking out the stalls.

†

Emma was shocked at Rayne's sudden departure. Pushing away from the table, she rushed to the door Rayne had just walked through.

"Rayne what's wrong? What did I do or say?" she shouted after her.

Rayne ignored her. Emma followed her into the barn.

"Just leave me alone, I don't want to talk right now," Rayne cried.

Emma stopped dead in her tracks. Her mind replayed the events of the meal, trying to grasp what it was that had upset Rayne so much. With nothing coming to her confused mind, she turned and headed back to the small house and into the kitchen where she sat down in a daze.

"Damn it, Rayne Mathews, I don't know what your problem is, but if you want to act as if that's how you want things, so be it," she said aloud as she stood and began picking up dishes and slamming them down. Once she finished the task of cleaning the kitchen, she moved to the bedroom. Her eyes went to the bed they had shared the night before. She grew warm at the memories and her body and heart reacted to what she remembered. Then she remembered Rayne's sudden coldness at breakfast. With a firm shake of her head, she uttered, "No. I will not pretend that was anything other than her just using me. She ain't no better than a man, thinking women of my lot in life is theirs for their pleasure. Well, you go ahead and enjoy memories of last night, Rayne, I promise it won't happen again," Emma ranted.

She tore the sheets off the bed so she could wash them.

†

The morning's work was long and hot and by the time she decided it was time to head in for lunch Rayne had finally sorted through her feelings and realized she owed Emma an apology. With a frowning face she rode Samson home, rehearsing how she would approach Emma. Once she turned the horse loose in the corral she headed to the house. She walked in expecting to see Emma and was surprised when she saw only one plate on the table. In an instant, she had forgotten that apology she was going to make and stormed back out of the house.

Chapter Twenty-seven

Emma heard the door open and Rayne walk into the kitchen then she heard the door slam again. With a tear in her eye, she lowered her head. *What did she expect, that I would be standing there with a smile waiting for her? After this morning...oh, I don't think so.*

So why are you crying, the tiny voice in her head asked.

"I don't know. Maybe because last night was so wonderful and I thought it was the same way for her," Emma answered aloud.

Emma was too busy thinking angry, painful thoughts that she didn't hear the door open or the foot-steps before it was too late. She turned when she heard the deep laugh. Emma backed up as her heart sank and fear started to paralyze her.

"So this is where you headed off to. Started a right nice household here, did ya? Sooo, you two....should have known any woman showing up to claim her family's ranch without a husband would be unnatural."

"What do you want here, Sprigs?" Emma tried to sound strong.

"Well, I came looking for that bitch, but since I found you instead, I suppose you'll do." Sprigs said as he approached her.

Emma looked at the door and thought she might be able to make it if she ran.

Sprigs' strong arms caught her, however, and once she was in his arms, Sprigs brought his mouth down to Emma's lips.

Emma pushed and tried to avoid the kiss but was unsuccessful.

When Sprigs pulled back, he was smiling. "Now that is how a man kisses and you know you enjoyed it. Let me show something that bitch could never show you."

He shoved Emma toward the bedroom.

†

Rayne spent the afternoon trying to get her mind off the previous night and her sudden doubts of the morning, and she wasn't finding it easy to concentrate. She finally gave up and decided to head back to the house and apologize to Emma and hopefully set things right.

"Emma, where are you? We need to talk," Rayne said as she walked into the house. When Emma didn't answer, she wandered into the bedroom looking for her. What she found angered her beyond words.

Emma lay on the bed with blood covering her face and her clothes ripped from her body.

"Oh my God, Emma, what happened? Who did this to you?" she cried as she ran to the bed.

"Spr…igs, I couldn't stop him, Rayne. I'm so sorry… I tried…God knows I tried. He was just too strong."

"Shh…oh God, I should have been closer to the house." Rayne briskly walked to the basin and got a washcloth wet then hurried back to clean Emma's face so she could assess the damage.

"I need to take you to the doc and make sure you're not hurt. I'll be right back." Rayne leaned down and kissed Emma's cheek.

She wasted no time hitching the horses to the wagon and leading them to the front of the house. Anger was surging in her body and she needed to keep it under control until the doc saw to Emma. "Then I will take you on, Sprigs and you *will* be sorry."

Inside, Rayne strapped on the holster with the pearl handled colt pistols that she had taken when she left Boston.

With a deep breath, she entered the bedroom and when she saw Emma, her heart broke.

"He will pay." She balled both her hands and ground her teeth.

Rayne wrapped Emma in a blanked before slipping her arms under Emma and lifting her off the bed. Emma was crying.

"I've got you," Rayne soothed. "The doc will fix you up."

"Oh, Rayne, it was so awful. I couldn't fight him."

"Emma, sweetheart, what all did Sprigs say to you?" Rayne asked gently. She felt the need to know fighting with not wanting to know equally in her heart.

"Rayne, he…he is evil. I don't know. I think he said the same would happen to you and that you should just give him what he wants."

"What does he want? God, he's never asked for anything,"

"The ranch…you…he said all your troubles would stop if you gave him the ranch."

"That will never happen." Rayne's anger was spilling out into her words finally.

"Rayne, why are you wearing your guns? Please tell me you aren't gonna go looking for trouble."

"Em, Sprigs has done something he never should have done and I aim to see him pay for it."

At those words Emma began crying harder.

Rayne tightened her arms around Emma, and pulled her close. "I've gotta set him straight. What's mine is mine and he ain't got no right to any of it. What he did to you is wrong and the law ain't gonna do anything about it so I have to."

"Please, Rayne, don't."

"I got to…I got to protect what's mine, otherwise someone else will think they can do the same thing and I can't have that happen."

Emma cried. "I don't want to lose you."

†

The wagon pulled up to the doc's place in town and Rayne tied the horses to the hitching post. She helped Emma down before sweeping Emma into her arms and carrying her into the office.

The doctor looked at Rayne then at the woman wrapped in her arms. "What happened?"

"Sprigs paid a visit to my place. Judging from the looks of her clothing, he beat Emma then had his way with her… ." Rayne couldn't contain the rage inside her.

"Is that true, Emma?"

"Yes." Emma began crying again.

"Well, come on back. Let's get you cleaned up and see what damage he's done to ya,"

"Doc, keep an eye on her. I got some business to tend to."

"Sure. Rayne, if you're doin' what I'm thinkin', reconsider. Sprigs is quick as a snake and he don't do anything fair."

"Thanks for the warning, Doc. Emma, I'll be back soon." Rayne kissed her tenderly then turned and walked back out the door.

✝

Rayne walked down the street toward the saloon, knowing she would find the bastard there. Her blood boiled, her heart raced, and she felt sick to her stomach at the thought of having to face the man. She had never believed completely that all her troubles at the ranch were from Sprigs' hands but, thinking on it all, it now made sense. Well, so be it, she wasn't about to part with the ranch that she loved nor was she gonna turn a blind eye to what the man did to the woman she loved. *Sprigs was gonna pay.*

✝

The saloon was lively with music and laughter. When Rayne walked in, it slowly came to an eerie silence. Sprigs, who was standing at the bar bragging about his early afternoon adventure, turned with a smile on his face and looked at Rayne.

"Well, if it ain't Rayne Mathews. Tell ya what, why don't you leave your ranch to me and take your unnatural self out of this town. We don't like nor want your kind here."

Rayne remembered what Alice had said about people whispering and having to hide. Rayne forced herself to be strong, "My ranch is exactly that…mine. As for the rest of my life that ain't none of your business nor is it that of anyone else in this town. Now, what you done to Emma, that is my business and I intend to call you out on it."

"You bitch, you think you can come in here and tell me what I can and can't do? Ask that little whore about it. I'll bet you anything she enjoyed havin' a man inside her. I know I sure as hell enjoyed bein' there. Oh, that get to ya there? Did it? Knowing you can never do for a woman what I can. No, no that ain't what hit you. You got a thing for that little whore, don't you, and you don't like that she enjoyed me."

Rayne buried her rage. "Sprigs, stay away from

me, my ranch, and Emma or I swear to God you'll be sorry."

"You bitch. That land should be mine along with your little whore. And I'll have them both!"

Sprigs face was red and his lips snarled as he drew on Rayne. Before he even cleared leather, the bullet from Rayne's gun struck him straight in the heart and he fell dead.

With tears of anger and pain, Rayne holstered her gun and turned toward the swinging doors just as the sheriff came running in.

Rayne stopped next to the Sheriff.

"Rayne, you want to tell me what happened here?"

"Tom, he drew on me, raped Emma, and was the one behind all the problems at the ranch."

"Boys, it true that Sprigs drew on Rayne here?"

The answer was a loud round of agreement.

"Any of you boys that worked for him know of the attempted rustlings over at the Rocking M Ranch? Keep in mind, ain't no crime been committed so you're all safe if ya speak up."

Several of the men who worked for Sprigs spoke up giving Tom all the information he needed to clear Rayne of any charges of murder. He motioned her out the saloon door.

Rayne walked out of the saloon toward the doc's office and a tearful Emma met her half way. "I couldn't wait to have your arms around me again," she said, staring into Rayne's eyes.

The two walked side by side to the wagon and

home, where they knew they would replace all the ug-
ly memories with happy ones that would last a lifetime.

Chapter Twenty-eight

Six weeks later Rayne was still holding Emma each night and listening as she sobbed herself to sleep. Rayne wanted to lash out and express her anger and would often go out into the canyon and scream as loud as she could until her throat hurt so bad she had to stop. What happened to Emma was brutal and even though she had killed Sprigs, the rage was still there.

Emma deserves better and I'm going to see to it that she gets that.

After doing her chores, Rayne walked out of the barn and made her way to the creek so she could wash up before going into the house. Her mind was working all the time trying to figure out what she could do that would make Emma feel safe and loved. Although Emma allowed her to hold her sometimes, she discouraged anything further. She remembered keenly their conversation from the night before…

"I'm dirty now, that man saw to that. How could anyone want to be with me in that way, Rayne?" Emma cried clutching the sheet across her neck.

"Emma, what that man did to you wasn't your fault…you are not to blame."

"How can you say that? I went willing with him in the saloon so of course he thought I'd like it again."

"No, no that isn't so. He was an evil man and you did nothing to encourage him. It was *Hank* who pushed you to go with him."

Emma shook her head. "I'm too tired to talk about this now. I just don't want you to hold me now…he made me dirty."

Rayne had forcibly wrapped her arms around Emma. "I love you," she had whispered.

Now, Rayne was determined to romance Emma and make her know how much she loved her. The only question was how. Rayne was at a loss as to how to get through to Emma.

Whatever you do, go slow, don't scare her any more than she already is.

"Emma, I need to ride out to the canyon to check on the herd. Why don't you go with me? I bet we can make it one more beautiful day. It won't be long before snow hits."

"I don't know…do you really want me to go with you?" Emma's eyes looked at the floor. She had grown gaunt and pale due to a new, poor appetite.

"Are you kidding? Of course I want you to go with me. We can pack a lunch and eat on the trail, it'll be nice."

"I…okay. I'll put something together."

"Great. I'll go saddle up Samson and Delilah and be right back." Rayne walked quickly away.

Outside, Rayne was smiling as she saddled the horses. Her mind jumbled with thoughts on how to start to break through the wall that Emma had put up.

Rayne came into the house, grabbed her guns, and strapped them around her hips. When she walked into the kitchen, she caught Emma's smile and it warmed her heart. "Hey, ya about ready? I got the horses outside ready to go. What do you need me to do?"

"If you want to pack these in the saddle bags that would be a big help."

"What do we have?" Rayne took in a deep breath. "It smells like a right fine meal."

"Well we have ham and biscuits, a couple of slices of pie, and some apples."

"Mmm, sounds delicious. What do you say about gettin' on our horses and just riding until we find a good spot to stop and eat?"

"Let's go." Emma's eyes rested on Rayne's waist and she shivered. "Why are you wearing your guns? Do you expect trouble?"

"No…not at all, just wanna be safe, okay?"

Emma sucked in a deep breath as if trying not to allow the fear to get to her. She nodded and turned toward the front door.

Rayne and Emma's ride to the canyon was filled with the chatter of two friends.

"It's beautiful here, isn't it?" Rayne said as they rode into the canyon.

"It is beautiful. Is the whole property this beautiful?"

"Yes, we have meadows and there are spots along the creek that are amazing."

"You really love the ranch, don't you?" Emma asked.

"Yeah, I do, it's the only place I've ever felt at home."

"Why?" Emma asked, waiting for Rayne to explain her comment.

It seems as if Sprigs never happened. Rayne couldn't stop the smile the thought caused.

In the canyon, Rayne found a nice clearing and they stopped. Emma spread a blanket while Rayne fetched their meal out of the saddlebags. The two settled into a nice relaxing lunch where the easy conversation of before continued and Emma actually smiled again.

"So what were you like as a child?" Emma asked.

With a laugh Rayne answered, "Stubborn, precocious. My aunt and uncle would tell you I was a handful. Always into this or that."

"Really, I can't imagine that," Emma said, laughing.

"Yeah, one time when I was about eight, I suppose, I decided I wanted to ride one of the horses and tried to saddle him myself. I got the blanket and saddle on and was just getting the reins on when Uncle Luke caught me. Instead of bein' mad, he helped me finish and went for a ride with me."

"Sounds like you *were* a handful. I wish I had known you then." Emma eased herself into a comfortable position next to Rayne.

With the fresh air and a full stomach Emma found herself relaxed and at ease and lay down with her head on Rayne's lap. Rayne began stroking Emma's hair back and Emma could see the joy on her face. Emma felt safe and let her eyes close.

After an hour, Rayne gently shook Emma's shoulder and she woke with a start.

"Shh, it's okay, you're safe."

Emma smiled, finally realizing anew the truth of those words. She would always be safe and protected by Rayne.

Together, they packed up the remains of their lunch and packed up the saddlebags, which Rayne eased over the saddle. Once finished, she walked over to Emma and brushed the hair out of her eyes.

When Rayne gently leaned in to place a light kiss on her lips, Emma didn't push her away. The warm lips touching hers made her feel warm and the flutter in her stomach that she always associated with Rayne was back. She welcomed the kiss and felt bereft when Rayne pulled away.

"We should get going'," Rayne said.

"Yeah, I suppose we should." Emma couldn't hide the disappointment she felt.

Rayne helped Emma mount Delilah and climbed on Samson. She looked over at Emma and smiled. "Ready?"

"Yes."

Together they went farther into the canyon and let their horses meander in and around the cattle.

"Oh my, Rayne, I never imagined it would be this beautiful."

Emma's eyes fell on the trees high up at the top of a rock wall just turning with a blush of the autumn color to come. "The colors of the trees are already stunning."

Emma closed her eyes and drew in a deep breath of the air. "Living my life at the saloon, I never saw anything like this. My view was pretty narrow."

"Emma, you don't need to ever go back there again or worry over anyone hurting you. I'm sorry I was being such a fool that day and ran away from you and my feelings for you."

"No. No, Rayne, it was never your fault. I was too sensitive and imagined things that never were."

"So did I…had I only stopped to think, Sprigs would never have hurt you again…I wouldn't have let him."

Emma felt the now familiar tightening in her chest with the mention of the man's name. She looked down the canyon and tried to see if she could pick out where they had eaten their lunch—the place where Rayne had kissed her.

"I wish I could stop the memories," she whispered. She looked at Rayne forcing her tears back. "You deserve so much better than me."

Rayne nudged Samson around so he was side by side with Delilah. "You are all I will ever want." She reached out and tenderly stroked Emma's check. "I've been waiting for you all my life…I love you, Emma."

Emma looked at Rayne as she shivered from Rayne's touch. "You shouldn't," she whispered

"Oh, Emma, what can I do to make you see that it was Sprigs who all the blame should go to? You did nothing to encourage him to do what he did to you. I know that in my heart…please believe me."

A slight smile curved Emma's lips. "I do believe you here," Emma placed her hand over her heart, "I just need to believe it here." She touched her head.

Rayne reached out and took Emma's hand. "Come on, let's go home."

"Home. I like the sound of that."

Emma's heart filled with joy and she began to heal.

Rayne said she loved me, filled her mind.

The ride back was companionable, leaving her feeling as good as if Sprigs had never entered her life.

Back at the house, the feeling continued. Emma managed to keep the memories at bay and let the present just happen. For the first time in weeks she helped with chores and then went in and got dinner for the two of them. She even ate. After dinner, Rayne helped with the dishes and the two sat in their chairs in the living area. While Rayne read, Emma mended one of Rayne's shirts.

It was only later, in bed, that Rayne knew the memories still haunted Emma as she cried herself to sleep. Rayne just held her, whispering that she was safe and no one would hurt her again.

Hours later, Rayne was still wide-awake trying to figure out how to get past the walls Emma had put up. At least it cracked a little when Emma had allowed her to kiss her.

Rayne still had to battle her guilt about that day too. She never should have left her alone. *Today she was able to forget for a little while...and so did I. Maybe that's how we both do it... just one day at a time and figure new ways to make each day special.*

Over the next few weeks, Rayne brought small gifts for Emma when she had to ride into town or she would do simple things to help Emma. Most of all, she never pressured Emma for more than she was willing or ready to give. With a tender kiss each night, along with an ear willing to listen and a shoulder for Emma to cry on, Rayne never wavered in her devotion to Emma. In that time, she realized that she needed to take her own advice and let go of her own guilt about that day.

✝

One evening as they sat in front of the fire, Emma looked at Rayne and saw her face bathed in the gentle glow from the flame.

She's so beautiful, she thought. *Why am I so afraid? She has been so gentle and kind to me yet I push her away. I'm not being fair to her.*

Emma remembered the one night they made love and how her body had come alive under Rayne's touch. She recalled how safe she felt in the cocoon of Rayne's arms. She wanted to feel that way again.

"Rayne, I know I haven't been fair to you, I'm sorry for that."

What do you mean?" Rayne lifted her eyes and stared at Emma.

"You're so kind to me and you've shown such patience and I know you want more."

"I would never push you or force you for more than you're willing to give, Em."

"I know that and I love you for that. I still feel like I'm not being fair."

"You love me?"

Emma nodded.

"Em, I love you with all my heart and I would never do anything to hurt you. I would die before I'd let anything bad happen to you again."

"I know you would. You've shown me that. You never get angry with me when I know you want more than a kiss. Thank you for that." Tears fell from her eyes. "You really aren't like him."

Rayne stood, knelt in front of Emma, and wiped away the tears. "Em, please don't cry anymore. I hate it when I see your tears, I hate knowing you're in pain."

Rayne wrapped her arms around Emma in comfort and laid her head in Emma's lap. Before she knew it, Emma had lifted her head and was kissing her. It started out soft and gentle but soon grew into a deep, soul-searing kiss.

Rayne, not breaking the connection of their lips, put her arms around Emma's waist and they stood together. The kiss created that sweet tightening that Rayne had squelched ever since the incident so many weeks ago.

Soon she felt the fiery passion rising in herself and in Emma. For far too long she had kept a tight rein on those feelings. The kiss lasted into the bedroom only stopping as they undressed one another. Together they fell onto the mattress where once again they expressed the love that spanned lifetimes.

Long after they fell asleep, tangled in one another's arms, the continuing glow of their love kept them safe and warm.

About the Author

Dannie Marsden

Let me introduce myself, I am Dannie, a butch-identified writer. I am committed to a beautiful woman, have three wonderful children and one adorable granddaughter.

I started writing about ten years ago and of course, my stories are centered on, what else...beautiful lesbian women. I try to write about strong women with vulnerabilities and soft caring who compliment, understand and support them. I hope I convey the many levels women have and the beauty of each level.

E-Books, Limited First Edition Print, Printed Books,
Free e-books

Visit our website for more publications available
online.

http://www.affinityebooks.com

Published by Affinity E-Book Press NZ Ltd

Canterbury, New Zealand

Registered company 2517228